Dark Night of the Soul

Journey to the Heart of God

By Joseph B. Lumpkin

For information and assistance for first-time authors, address inquiries to:
Fifth Estate Publishers, Post Office Box 116, Blountsville, AL 35031.

Third Edition

Printed on acid-free paper

Library of Congress Control No: 2004103051

ISBN 0-9746336-3-1

Fifth Estate 02/2006

Introduction

For those who tend to read books through in a single sitting, and for those who are interested in light reading, or the "thought for the day," this book is not for you. It will add a level of frustration in your life that can be avoided by placing this work back on a shelf and walking away. However, if you are seeking a deeper meaning in your life; if you feel alone, lost, or unsure in your faith; if you are desperately seeking God Himself, this book will call to you. It is not an easy read, but then, faith and hope are not easily explained. It is best to read a few pages or thoughts at a time and then pause to let them seep into your heart. Reach down into your soul and contemplate their full effects. Search the length and breadth of the consequences of your beliefs and faith and seek the very heart of God and His grace in your lives through the words you read. Take your time. God will be there, waiting. The journey is not an easy one. It takes heart-wrenching emptiness to be filled with only Him.

Joseph Lumpkin
March 2004

TO KNOW HIM

Spiritual life in the West has become superficial and narcissistic, a diluted pseudo Christianity mixed with Eastern occultism, so bogged down in doctrine and church laws as to be legalistic by nature and impudent in force. It is possible the demise of contemplative worship in the West is a direct result of an ever-accelerating lifestyle. We now live in a world where there are more and more people who live in greater and greater personal isolation, or possibly the better word is insulation. We interact as if we have a thickening armor over our hearts. We develop a skin to emotionally protect us. The "skin" keeps indignities forced on us by our society and our fellow man from harming us but it is affecting our spiritual lives. In the Christian church of today there is lack of commitment. We want to get to the conclusion before we get through the starting gate. Our fast-food religion focuses on one or two exciting and entertaining hours a week. There are no more voices crying in the wilderness because the wilderness of our hearts is left unexplored and there are none who dare venture into the dark regions of the soul. God waits for us in the quiet wilderness of our hearts. What shall we do?

The future of Christianity may lie solely in the mystical tradition, which demands a direct and personal relationship with God. Any hope of true salvation and personal growth in Christianity hinges on the depth of our relationship with Christ himself. The entire Christian faith is based on a direct and unique connection between the individual and God. In this aspect, Christianity is a most mystical and dynamic faith. The Christian faith demands union and communion with the creator wherein He teaches us, guides us, and loves us. Through meditation, adoration, and prayer we are joined with Him and transformed from within. Such love and transformation engendered by this relationship can reunite Christians with the power, courage, and glory needed to survive in a world which is becoming increasingly hostile to them.

With most people, and sadly, with most Christians, a crucial gap remains between God and man. What is needed is not the teaching of doctrine, law, or church tradition, nor is it any social or moral message. We need a heart-to-heart dialogue with God. We need and long for a relationship with our creator in which He loves and teaches us as a father would a child. A child knows he is loved by the kiss on his cheek, the words, the touch, and the embrace. It is in this type of communion we "know" God. He has bid us come, but the modern church has forgotten the path. It is still there, beneath the hedges of religion and pride. The hedges must be cleared away to find the path.

One may think in reading this work it is a treatise against doctrine or opposed to theology. One may think it is purely a work calling us back to some simplistic, emotional, or childish view of faith. This could not be further from the truth. This book is a call for balance, and a summoning of us inward and away from the superficial, outward-looking worship of today. This path is not simplistic, but it is simple. It is not childish, but it is childlike. It is not emotional but it gives way to a path, which leads to a depth beyond empty knowledge and passing emotion. This path will lead us to the heart of knowing. There we will see faith has been waiting all the while. The formula of the worship of today is equal parts of emotional gratification, superficial study of scripture, and adherence to rules of denomination. We have neglected the one thing that stands as the banner of Christianity - a relationship with God through Christ our Lord. The Christian faith is the only religion in which God seeks out man. God seeks to engage man in a relationship that is emotional and unique. What a wonder, to have a relationship with the creator.

It may be argued the Jewish faith encourages a relationship of this type. However, in Christ we have a God who has shed his heavenly state in order to seek out man. He extends his hand to us so we may see that He understands us. God demonstrates this by living as we live, suffering as we suffer, and experiencing life as only man can in order that He, God, might have compassion (a word meaning to suffer together) on us and empathy (meaning to feel the same thing) with us so that we may know He knows us and we may have a personal relationship with Him. For, if God is omniscient He would have already known what it was like to be man, but we could not have conceived of His knowledge.

In Christ we have the hero-God-king who relinquished everything including His life in order to seek, love, and save His people. There is nothing left emotionally undone in this formula God has given us. It is in the church of today the formula becomes incorrect. Denominationalism has supplanted Scripture and following a set of rules has become more important than knowing He who made them. It is most essential to seek and know God, and to love Him, if we are to be changed by His love into His image. Only in this marvelous transformation can we hope to come close to doing what He has asked: Love God with your whole being. Love your fellow man as yourself. Doctrine and Scripture are to keep us on a path that we might better know Him. Theology serves to clarify ones' beliefs in order that they may be articulated.

But the study of theology does not serve to edify man. It seems almost arrogant to endeavor to study He who is omnipotent and omniscient. Learning scripture and points of doctrine serves to enhance our knowledge, but not our heart. We seek to gain insight into God's patterns and personality through study. This is admirable to a point; however, time may be best served by being in His presence. To know Him is always better than to study Him.

To better know Him is the purpose of this meager work.

PART ONE

A GIFT OF LOVE

Interior experiences, those that are spiritual or mystical, lack common language. There are no tangible points of reference neither in item or place that we may compare and establish mutual terms. It is because of this lack of spiritual language that the mystical experience cannot be easily explained. It is alluded to, pointed at, and explained by allegory and metaphor at best. In this context, it is marriage and love, both physical and emotional, which come closest to the mystical experience. On these experiences we shall rely in order to discuss the indescribable.

Mysticism – The doctrine that communion with God and a knowledge of the divine essence may be attained independent of the senses or processes of reason through intuition and insight; hence, the ecstasy of those who claim they have had insight or vision bringing them into spiritual union with the eternal and giving them knowledge of the supernatural.
Webster's New School & Office Dictionary

Doctrine – That which is taught: The principles, belief, or dogma of any church, sect, or party.
Webster's New School & Office Dictionary

Communion – Intercourse; fellowship; common possession; a religious body; partaking of the Eucharist.   Webster's New School & Office Dictionary

What a terrible blessing and frightening gift has been given man that he should possess such great capacity to love and such vast ignorance of how to love. What divine urgings drive us to seek out in others that part of Him we so dimly recognize and that our hearts would respond so joyously to His reflection we glimpse in the face of our lover. Oh, feral heart who would settle for the corporeal

1

image but refuse the spiritual source when both are offered so openly. So saddening is the need to touch and feel and taste the beloved that it goads us like animals down the wrong path, settling only for someone to hold and shunning the higher and more pure love of Him who created the very object of our mortal love.

This is a short and barren path, on which we seek love with our whole being and settle for the echo of His voice heard distorted in the mundane love of this world. Why do we turn our hearts away from the clarion call of God beckoning us home? Possibly it is because we have no insight into what we are missing. The plan of family is set in heaven to teach us in types and symbols the relationship of Christ to man and man to Christ. It is a sacred lesson learned on earth. Husbands are told to love their wives as Christ loved the church. Wives are told to be obedient to their husbands. Children are protected, nurtured, and loved. Marriage is the deepest exercise of spiritual application in secular life… if we get it right.

EPH 5:22 Wives, submit yourselves unto your own husbands, as unto the Lord. 23 For the husband is the head of the wife, even as Christ is the head of the church: and he is the Savior of the body. 24 Therefore as the church is subject unto Christ, so let the wives be to their own husbands in every thing. 25 Husbands, love your wives, even as Christ also loved the church, and gave himself for it; 26 That he might sanctify and cleanse it with the washing of water by the word, 27 That he might present it to himself a glorious church, not having spot, or wrinkle, or any such thing; but that it should be holy and without blemish. 28 So ought men to love their wives as their own bodies. He that loveth his wife loveth himself.

MAR 10:13 And they brought young children to him, that he should touch them: and his disciples rebuked those that brought them. 14 But when Jesus saw it, he was much displeased, and said unto them, Suffer the little children to come unto me, and forbid them not: for of such is the kingdom of God. 15 Verily I say unto you, Whosoever shall not receive the

2

kingdom of God as a little child, he shall not enter therein.16 And he took them up in his arms, put his hands upon them, and blessed them.

We love and cherish one another. We bind our hearts together as lover and beloved. We seek and find a spiritual nature in the relationships of lover, spouse, and family. It is what God intended us to have. Yet, God intended more for us. There is still an emptiness and void unfilled. We love and are unsure of being loved. We are loved but fall short of loving. We wait for that time we may feel possessed and protected by love. We look to the world, but our hearts wait for God. It is not loving or being loved that is needed. We wait on love itself to come. We wait, but He is already here.

PSA 139:7 Whither shall I go from thy spirit? or whither shall I flee from thy presence? 8 If I ascend up into heaven, thou art there: if I make my bed in hell, behold, thou art there. 9 If I take the wings of the morning, and dwell in the uttermost parts of the sea; 10 Even there shall thy hand lead me, and thy right hand shall hold me.

Somehow, our hearts know Him but we cannot see Him. His presence is felt, His spirit is heard, but our eyes are blind, our ears are deaf to the soft rustle of His steps. In the search for love, our hearts frantically scan the faces of those around us. Are you He for whom I search? Are you the Lord? We look into the eyes of everyone passing, testing each one, until we can say, "I look at your face and I see God." When our hearts recognize the face of God in another, we call it love and there we abide. The love of our spouse, at the highest level, is a reflection of the spiritual love we seek in God. The bonding we seek from our spouse is a shadow of a higher need, to bond with God. We love but still, we are not filled. How can the darkened light of our souls illuminate the corners of another's heart? It is a relationship with God that we seek. We await Him who is love. Our relationships with others are divinely inspired by the template of God calling us to a communion with Him. Marriage is sacred. It is based on a divine plan of shadows and types from God showing us how we should love Him and be loved by Him.

3

SOL 1:15 Behold, thou art fair, my love; behold, thou art fair; thou hast doves' eyes. 16 Behold, thou art fair, my beloved, yea, pleasant: also our bed is green. 17 The beams of our house are cedar, and our rafters of fir. 2:1 I am the rose of Sharon, and the lily of the valleys. 2 As the lily among thorns, so is my love among the daughters. 3 As the apple tree among the trees of the wood, so is my beloved among the sons. I sat down under his shadow with great delight, and his fruit was sweet to my taste. 4 He brought me to the banqueting house, and his banner over me was love.

SON 2:10 My beloved spake, and said unto me, Rise up, my love, my fair one, and come away. 11 For, lo, the winter is past, the rain is over and gone;12 The flowers appear on the earth; the time of the singing of birds is come, and the voice of the turtle is heard in our land; 13 The fig tree putteth forth her green figs, and the vines with the tender grape give a good smell. Arise, my love, my fair one, and come away. 14 O my dove, that art in the clefts of the rock, in the secret places of the stairs, let me see thy countenance, let me hear thy voice; for sweet is thy voice, and thy countenance is comely.

SON 5:2 I sleep, but my heart waketh: it is the voice of my beloved that knocketh, saying, Open to me, my sister, my love, my dove, my undefiled: for my head is filled with dew, and my locks with the drops of the night.

We seek a deep and abiding communion with another because the desire is placed in us. Relationships of husband and wife are driven to a spiritual depth by the same yearning of togetherness set in us by God for Himself. The pattern of true friendship and holy marriage are the worldly symbols of the heavenly marriage between the believer and Christ. Sex becomes spiritual in this context...the ultimate attempt to commune, share, love, and be one in heart and soul. Yet, in our hearts we are being called home to a place we have never been. We pine for a friend and lover we have barely met. Only He can fill our hearts and souls completely. Only in Him can we rest. Only then will our spirits be at peace.

It is not that we do not love friends or family, but there is a higher love and a deeper calling making us know we are not yet fulfilled, not yet at peace, not yet at rest, not yet free of the emptiness that so graciously plagues our souls.

What devastating mercy and vicious grace has been given man that he would receive by some charity of the Spirit of God this disease of sorrow that only God can cure. Only in this relationship called Christianity does God place a hook in our hearts and draw us homeward. Only here do we have the fisher of men. The great physician and loving Father listens for our call. "Lord, what must I do to be saved?" It is the question that starts the journey of a lifetime as God answers in lessons of love for the rest of our lives.

ACTS 16:29 Then he called for a light, and sprang in, and came trembling, and fell down before Paul and Silas, 30 And brought them out, and said, Sirs, what must I do to be saved? 31 And they said, Believe on the Lord Jesus Christ, and thou shalt be saved, and thy house. 32 And they spake unto him the word of the Lord, and to all that were in his house. 33 And he took them the same hour of the night, and washed their stripes; and was baptized, he and all his, straightway.

This relationship is a marriage mystical and eternal. Christ has assumed his rightful place as both redeemer and husband. He is the spiritual head and high priest of the family of God. He is the bridegroom of the believers. He is the beloved.

REV 21:2 And I John saw the holy city, new Jerusalem, coming down from God out of heaven, prepared as a bride adorned for her husband. 3 And I heard a great voice out of heaven saying,

Behold, the tabernacle of God is with men, and he will dwell with them, and they shall be his people, and God himself shall be with them, and be their God.

REV 22:17 And the Spirit and the bride say, Come. And let him that heareth say, Come. And let him that is athirst come. And whosoever will, let him take the water of life freely.

Brethren; I am homesick for a place that I have never been but I know a man who knows the way.   W.R. Lumpkin

COUNT IT ALL GRACE

When starting the mystical journey it may seem appropriate to bring all of your sins of the past up once again before God and confess all you have confessed before. It may seem good to remember yourself in light of how you were as a sinner. While it is true we are low, unworthy wretches, even this state and all sins are couched in grace. All trials and all sins are not only covered under His grace but are part of His grace. This does not diminish our sins in any way. It does not elevate us spiritually one inch, yet it does show us His magnificent and loving heart. For every step and misstep, all pain and tribulation brought us here to His feet and without any of them we would not be here for such a time as this. Only distress, physical or emotional, forces us to consider our path and only pain of this sort detours us to try other ways. We learn from our mistakes but should not be kept down by them. We repent and must leave the sorrow of our past deeds behind us.

Don't be troubled when you meditate on the greatness of your former sins, but rather know that God's grace is so much greater in magnitude that it justifies the sinner and absolves the wicked. Quotations from Cyril of Alexandria (Commentary on the Gospel of St. Luke)

Such a sweet and wonderful balance is maintained between remembering our wretched state and seeking to forget even ourselves in our search for God.

...if any man or woman should think to come to contemplation without many sweet meditations... on their own wretched state, on the passion, the kindness and the great goodness and the worthiness of God, they will certainly be deceived and fail in their purpose. At the same time, those men and women who are long practiced in these meditations must leave them aside, put them down

and hold them far under the cloud of forgetting, if they are ever to pierce the cloud of unknowing between them and their God. From The Cloud of Unknowing

I count it all grace that He knew the path of my sinful steps even before He saved me and still, He saved me. I count it all grace that He somehow wove my freewill into His plan, knowing how low and undeserving I am for His love. I count it all grace, my sins, my strengths, my weaknesses, and all of my limitations are counted as a terrible and undeniable gift designed by God to work in conjunction with the path I walk to lead me homeward to Him. Known by God from before the beginning, knitted together in the womb by His hand, blessed with human frailties so deep and pervasive as to have cost the life of God himself, I was led to God's feet.

He who is Love has given me the gift of love. It was given for nothing I have done or been. I was sinful even while confessing my sin. There was no need to beg for love. He loves me more than life. There is nothing I may do to thank Him or repay Him except by my free will to accept this gift He gives that it not be given in vain.

ROM 5:17 For if by one man's offence death reigned by one; much more they which receive abundance of grace and of the gift of righteousness shall reign in life by one, Jesus Christ. 18 Therefore as by the offence of one judgment came upon all men to condemnation; even so by the righteousness of one the free gift came upon all men unto justification of life. 19 For as by one man's disobedience many were made sinners, so by the obedience of one shall many be made righteous. 20 Moreover the law entered, that the offence might abound. But where sin abounded, grace did much more abound: 21 That as sin hath reigned unto death, even so might grace reign through righteousness unto eternal life by Jesus Christ our Lord. 6:1 What shall we say then? Shall we continue in sin, that grace may abound? 2 God forbid. How shall we, that are dead to sin, live any longer therein?

ROM 6:14 For sin shall not have dominion over you: for ye are not under the law, but under grace. 15 What then? shall we sin, because we are not under the law, but under grace? God forbid. 16 Know ye not, that to whom ye yield yourselves servants to obey, his servants ye are to whom ye obey; whether of sin unto death, or of obedience unto righteousness?

For I have attempted to keep myself from sin and sinning and repeatedly failed, utterly. Trying to run or hide from my fallen nature and always finding me with me and never leaving or losing one iota of me, I gave up trying to change me and laid down before Him any hope of my own righteousness. I count myself the only sinner and have received firm rejection from the church, being unable, for any time, to stay me from sinning. Yet, I still feel His spirit welling up within me. But now, there is nowhere to go but to His heart, alone.

You do not have to be perfect. Perfection is not what Christianity is all about. You do your best and God does the "righteousing".   Dr. Gene Scott.

1CO 15:10 But by the grace of God I am what I am: and his grace which was bestowed upon me was not in vain; but I laboured more abundantly than they all: yet not I, but the grace of God which was with me.

2CO 4:14 Knowing that he which raised up the Lord Jesus shall raise up us also by Jesus, and shall present us with you. 15 For all things are for your sakes, that the abundant grace might through the thanksgiving of many redound to the glory of God. 16 For which cause we faint not; but though our outward man perish, yet the inward man is renewed day by day.

JAM 1:1 James, a servant of God and of the Lord Jesus Christ, to the twelve tribes, which are scattered abroad, greeting. 2 My brethren, count it all joy when ye fall into divers temptations; 3

Knowing this, that the trying of your faith worketh patience. 4 But let patience have her perfect work, that ye may be perfect and entire, wanting nothing.

ZEC 4:6   Then he answered and spake unto me, saying, This is the word of the LORD unto Zerubbabel, saying, Not by might, nor by power, but by my spirit, saith the LORD of hosts. 7 Who art thou, O great mountain? before Zerubbabel thou shalt become a plain: and he shall bring forth the headstone thereof with shoutings, crying, grace, grace unto it.

Having been shown His grace, by His grace, I at once saw my shortcomings and needs and was drawn to know a basic wrongness in me. I now hold on with my life, for my life, to the grace of God, knowing He who made me knew me and still loved me enough to woo me, with His prevenient grace, by His spirit, back to Him. And if He could and would do this, that by His longsuffering and forgiveness, He would keep loving me to the very end, seeing that He knew all I would be and do before He saved me. By doing this, He is keeping me for Himself until that day I may be made perfect, over there.

WHAT IS GRACE?

Only by the grace of God can salvation and the communion we seek take place. We may ask. We may beg. But, it is only in watchful waiting that we will receive. His grace is sufficient and the only vehicle by which salvation and communion with God is granted. But what is grace?

Grace is a blessing, a blessing that is undeserved, unsolicited and unexpected, a blessing that brings a sense of the divine order of things into our lives. The ways of grace are mysterious, we cannot always figure them out. But we know grace by its fruits, by the blessings of its works. We would expect to be startled when grace manifests itself. The opposite is true. It doesn't startle us at all, for grace is everywhere. We may not discern it; we may not recognize it for we are inclined to take it for granted.   "Living with Grace"   by Rev. Peter Fleck

If we are walking, dancing, eating, teaching, preaching, meditating, being, we are rid of the impediments which hinder our free movement. We are rid of all the obstacles that block us from being who we are meant to be. This is grace. A grace that indicates not an addition, but rather a subtraction and removal of those things that may hinder us from being who we are. This is grace.   Reverend Bill Clark

Grace "is an attitude on God's part that proceeds entirely from within Himself, and that is conditioned in no way by anything in the objects of His favor." Burton Scott Easton in The International Standard Bible Encyclopedia.

When a thing is said to be of 'grace' we mean that the recipient has no claim upon it, that it was in no-wise due him. It comes to him as pure charity, and, at first, unasked and undesired.   A.W. Pink Attributes of God

In a time before his death, Mr. McLaren, minister of the Tolboth church, said, "I am gathering together all my prayers, all my sermons, all my good deeds, all my ill deeds; and I am going to throw them all overboard and swim to glory on the plank of Free Grace."

There is one work which is right and proper for us to do, and that is the eradication of self. But however great this eradication and reduction of self may be, it remains insufficient if God does not complete it in us. For our humility is only perfect when God humbles us through ourselves. Only then are they and the virtue perfected, and not before.   Meister Eckhart

If I were good and holy enough to be elevated among the saints, then the people would discuss and question whether this was by grace or nature and would be troubled about it. But this would be wrong of them. Let God work in you, acknowledge that it is his work, and do not be concerned as to whether he achieves this by means of nature or beyond nature. Both nature and grace are his. What is it to you which means he best uses or what he performs in you or in someone else? He should work how and where and in what manner it suits him to do so. Meister Eckhart

The self-righteous, relying on the many good works he imagines he has performed, seems to hold salvation in his own hand, and considers Heaven as a just reward of his merits. In the bitterness of his zeal he exclaims against all sinners, and represents the gates of mercy as barred against them, and Heaven as a place to which they have no claim. What need have such self-righteous persons of a Saviour? They are already burdened with the load of their own merits. Oh, how long they bear the flattering load, while sinners divested of everything, fly rapidly on the wings of faith and love into their Saviour's arms, who freely bestows on them that which he has so freely promised! Jeanne-Marie Bouvier de la Motte-Guyon

Humility is a grace in the soul... It is indescribable wealth, a name and a gift from God. Learn from Me, He said; that is, not from an angel, not from a man, not from a book, but from Me, that is from My dwelling within you, from My illumination and action within you, for I am gentle and meek of heart in thought and in spirit, and your souls will find rest from conflicts and relief from evil thoughts.   John Climacus

Our activity consists of loving God and our fruition of enduring God and being penetrated by his love. There is a distinction between the love and fruition, as there is between God and his Grace. John Ruusbroec

Jesus, are you not my mother? Are you not even more than my mother? My human mother after all labored in giving birth to me only for a day or night; you, my tender and beautiful lord, labored for me over 30 years.   Marguerite of Oingt

We are only here and possess what we have because of the timing and grace of God. Whether we have little or we have much, we have it because of God. The love in our hearts and all things we have and feel are because He made us as we are. He sets our path and places us on the path at His time. The people we meet and places we go and thus the situations springing from them are in our lives

13

because we were born at such a time as this. Gratitude keeps our arrogance and pride in check. It assigns all of what we are and all we have to God who made all things and keeps them in existence. Gratitude is the balance point between God and man. Thankfulness is a measure of our dependence on God and our obedience to Him. It is the path that our prayers walk to get to God. Gratitude is how we approach Him. It is said there are only two things that motivate us to do things: desire and desperation. It is said, "gratitude comes from desire". This is the idea of some philosophers, but there is a higher gratitude not understood by the world.

There is a gratitude springing from the realization that one has no desires, no needs, nothing lacking. It is gratitude from epiphany. Insight brought on by grace enables us to see how God is providing our path and all things on it. It does not mean we have riches or even health, but that we are where we are supposed to be. Even in our lack or pain, we see somehow we are exactly where God would have us to be. It is the gratitude of knowing what we need to fulfill our purpose will be provided on God's path for God's purpose. All things are seen in a state of grace and balance and we are here for a purpose; God's purpose.

FAITH

Faith is the key we turn to enter through the door of salvation. It unlocks the door of heaven and the presence of God.

EPH 2:8 For by grace are ye saved through faith; and that not of yourselves: it is the gift of God: Not of works, lest any man should boast.

Faith is action based upon belief, sustained by confidence.   Dr Gene Scott

You may ask why I have chosen to discuss faith at this point in a book that is seemingly dedicated to knowing God in a personal sense. After all, knowing trumps faith, doesn't it? No. It does not. There will be times of darkness and trouble in our journey when we will doubt we ever heard the voice of God. It is in these times the faith will triumph. However, neither faith nor knowing can come first. God's grace must come first. God must first open our eyes to our own inadequacies and reveal to us our need for Him. God must draw us to Him in a sovereign act of grace. He must then give us the faith by which we are saved. Faith and Grace are the two powers yoked together to pull us out of this world and into eternity.

ROM 12:3 For I say, through the grace given unto me, to every man that is among you, not to think of himself more highly than he ought to think; but to think soberly, according as God hath dealt to every man the measure of faith.

Yes, even our faith is a gift from God. Faith is manifest in the act of believing in someone we have not yet met and believing He is who He said He is, the only begotten Son of God. Faith comes to us from God by grace. We worship Him but He enables us to do so. He enables us to believe. He gives us the faith to be saved. He opens our eyes and our hearts to His word and draws us by His spirit. It is by

15

faith we come to God and by faith we live. It is better to believe than to know, for knowing can be shaken in those times when we reach for God and cannot find Him. In those times He is silent and our souls are tested with darkness, it is only by faith we will survive. As a child whose father has left on a long journey, we no longer see Him, but we have faith He will return. We have faith He is there, still loving us. It is faith given as an act of love and grace that allows us to await His return.

HAB 2:3 For the vision is yet for an appointed time, but at the end it shall speak, and not lie: though it tarry, wait for it; because it will surely come, it will not tarry. 4 Behold, his soul which is lifted up is not upright in him: but the just shall live by his faith.

ACT 26:18 To open their eyes, and to turn them from darkness to light, and from the power of Satan unto God, that they may receive forgiveness of sins, and inheritance among them which are sanctified by faith that is in me.

ROM 1:16 For I am not ashamed of the gospel of Christ: for it is the power of God unto salvation to every one that believeth; to the Jew first, and also to the Greek. 17 For therein is the righteousness of God revealed from faith to faith: as it is written, The just shall live by faith.

ROM 3:21 But now the righteousness of God without the law is manifested, being witnessed by the law and the prophets; 22 Even the righteousness of God which is by faith of Jesus Christ unto all and upon all them that believe: for there is no difference: 23 For all have sinned, and come short of the glory of God; 24 Being justified freely by his grace through the redemption that is in Christ Jesus: ROM 3:25 Whom God hath set forth to be a propitiation through faith in his blood, to declare his righteousness for the remission of sins that are past, through the forbearance of God; 26 To declare, I say, at this time his righteousness: that he might be just, and the justifier of him which believeth in Jesus.

ROM 3:28 Therefore we conclude that a man is justified by faith without the deeds of the law.

ROM 4:16 Therefore it is of faith, that it might be by grace; to the end the promise might be sure to all the seed; not to that only which is of the law, but to that also which is of the faith of Abraham; who is the father of us all, ROM 4:23 Now it was not written for his sake alone, that it was imputed to him; 24 But for us also, to whom it shall be imputed, if we believe on him that raised up Jesus our Lord from the dead; 25 Who was delivered for our offences, and was raised again for our justification. 5:1 Therefore being justified by faith, we have peace with God through our Lord Jesus Christ: 2 By whom also we have access by faith into this grace wherein we stand, and rejoice in hope of the glory of God.

GAL 2:16 Knowing that a man is not justified by the works of the law, but by the faith of Jesus Christ, even we have believed in Jesus Christ, that we might be justified by the faith of Christ, and not by the works of the law: for by the works of the law shall no flesh be justified.

GAL 3:24 Wherefore the law was our schoolmaster to bring us unto Christ, that we might be justified by faith. 25 But after that faith is come, we are no longer under a schoolmaster. For ye are all the children of God by faith in Christ Jesus.

1TI 6:12 Fight the good fight of faith, lay hold on eternal life, whereunto thou art also called, and hast professed a good profession before many witnesses.

HEB 11:1 Now faith is the substance of things hoped for, the evidence of things not seen. 2 For by it the elders obtained a good report. 3 Through faith we understand that the worlds were framed by the word of God, so that things which are seen were not made of things which do appear. 4 By faith Abel offered unto God a more excellent sacrifice than Cain, by which he obtained witness that he was righteous, God testifying of his gifts: and by it he being dead yet speaketh. 5 By faith Enoch was

17

translated that he should not see death; and was not found, because God had translated him: for before his translation he had this testimony, that he pleased God. 6 But without faith it is impossible to please him: for he that cometh to God must believe that he is, and that he is a rewarder of them that diligently seek him.

HEB 11:7 By faith Noah, being warned of God of things not seen as yet, moved with fear, prepared an ark to the saving of his house; by the which he condemned the world, and became heir of the righteousness which is by faith. 8 By faith Abraham, when he was called to go out into a place which he should after receive for an inheritance, obeyed; and he went out, not knowing whither he went. 9 By faith he sojourned in the land of promise, as in a strange country, dwelling in tabernacles with Isaac and Jacob, the heirs with him of the same promise: 10 For he looked for a city which hath foundations, whose builder and maker is God. HEB 11:11 Through faith also Sara herself received strength to conceive seed, and was delivered of a child when she was past age, because she judged him faithful who had promised. 12 Therefore sprang there even of one, and him as good as dead, so many as the stars of the sky in multitude, and as the sand which is by the sea shore innumerable. 13 These all died in faith, not having received the promises, but having seen them afar off, and were persuaded of them, and embraced them, and confessed that they were strangers and pilgrims on the earth.

Even with this most holy of things, faith in God, one can supplant the creator with the creature and fall victim to believing in faith itself. If we place faith in our ability to have faith it lessens our perceived dependence on God. I say perceived dependence because we have just crossed the line into the great lie by thinking we can fulfill our needs and do it better than God. Faith in faith is not faith in God. If we do not fully understand our faith comes from God, given by Him in his measure to us, we can come to believe that we have some work or contribution in this faith of ours. This belief, added to the false concept that God must respond to faith, has yielded up a doctrine that is akin to witchcraft. The doctrine of many sects of Wicca states, "As My will, so may it be." This is not so different from the "hyper-faith" concept of having enough faith to compel God to act on behalf of the one with faith. One should always stretch a truth to see if it will break. If it breaks down it is not a truth. This one does not take much stretching to come apart and not much examination to see the cracks.

What ill-thought heresy would pit Christian against Christian in a battle of faith with God as a puppet in between? This is what would happen if the concept were to be practiced by two people competing for the same job, position, raise, or possession. What right have we to expect our prayers to change the mind or path of another person? Even God allows free will, yet some expect their prayers to influence others. Worldly perspective, arrogance, pride, and greed have brought the simple concept of faith and grace into a place of wish-craft bordering on witchcraft. The "Think and Grow Rich" idea of Napoleon Hill has made its way into our churches and has destroyed our view of God's faith, replacing it with faith in faith and faith in some ability of ours to wield a wand-like power contained in our belief in ourselves. Anything that takes our spiritual eyes off of Jesus as the only source of our salvation and spiritual power is wrong. To have Him we must rely on Him.

First, you must make Him your dwelling place.   Dr. Gene Scott

Our banner and cry should be, By faith alone through His grace.

FROM GOD, CHARITY OF HEART

There are two states in a man's life - love, and a call to be loved. We seek unconditional love because only through this God-like love we rest assured of being accepted with all sins and shortcomings that haunt us every waking hour and in our nightmares. It seems right that we would seek to deliver this kind of love to those closest to us such as our children, spouse, and friends. This kind of love flows from the heart of God. It flows through us to others.

Meaning of Agape': a · ga · pe   NOUN: 1. Christian Love as revealed in Jesus, seen as spiritual and selfless and a model for humanity. 2. Love that is spiritual, not sexual, in its nature. 3. Christianity in the early Christian Church, the love feast accompanied by Eucharistic celebration.

Agape' is God's pure unconditional Love and it's always used as such in the Bible. *Nancy Missler*

Agape' (noun) and *agapao* (verb) -- This is the word of Godly love. This special significance really comes in the New Testament period. *Agape'* is not found in secular literature, at least to any great extent, during the biblical period. The writers of the Septuagint use the noun some twenty times, but use the verb form over 250 times. In general terms, the Septuagint translators "invented" a new meaning for *agape'* by using it to replace the Hebrew *hesed*, a word meaning loving-kindness. Jude Ministries

Look closely at the difference in translations when it comes to the word agape'.

1CO 13:13 And now abideth faith, hope, charity (agape'), these three; but the greatest of these is charity. 14:1 Follow after charity (agape'), and desire spiritual gifts, but rather that ye may prophesy

20

1CO 13:13 And now abide faith, hope, love (agape'), these three; but the greatest of these is love (agape')

1CO 8:1 … Knowledge puffeth up, but charity (agape') edifieth. 2 And if any man think that he knoweth any thing, he knoweth nothing yet as he ought to know. 3 But if any man love God, the same is known of him.

1CO 13:1 Though I speak with the tongues of men and of angels, and have not charity, (agape') I am become as sounding brass, or a tinkling cymbal. 2 And though I have the gift of prophecy, and understand all mysteries, and all knowledge; and though I have all faith, so that I could remove mountains, and have not charity (agape'), I am nothing. 3 And though I bestow all my goods to feed the poor, and though I give my body to be burned, and have not charity (agape'), it profiteth me nothing. 4 Charity (agape') suffereth long, and is kind; charity (agape') envieth not; charity (agape') vaunteth not itself, is not puffed up, 5 Doth not behave itself unseemly, seeketh not her own, is not easily provoked, thinketh no evil; 6 Rejoiceth not in iniquity, but rejoiceth in the truth; 7 Beareth all things, believeth all things, hopeth all things, endureth all things. 8 Charity (agape') never faileth:…

So many things flow from the love of God in us. Actions reach out to others in compassion and giving that arise from the impulse of love planted so deeply in our hearts we cannot resist. By these acts, and by this love we shall know we are saved.

1PE 1:22 Seeing ye have purified your souls in obeying the truth through the Spirit unto unfeigned love of the brethren, see that ye love one another with a pure heart fervently: 23 Being born again, not of corruptible seed, but of incorruptible, by the word of God, which liveth and abideth for ever.

1JO 3:14 We know that we have passed from death unto life, because we love the brethren…

21

JAM 2:14 What doth it profit, my brethren, though a man say he hath faith, and have not works? can faith save him? 15 If a brother or sister be naked, and destitute of daily food, 16 And one of you say unto them, Depart in peace, be ye warmed and filled; notwithstanding ye give them not those things which are needful to the body; what doth it profit? 17 Even so faith, if it hath not works, is dead, being alone. 18 Yea, a man may say, Thou hast faith, and I have works: shew me thy faith without thy works, and I will shew thee my faith by my works. 19 Thou believest that there is one God; thou doest well: the devils also believe, and tremble. 20 But wilt thou know, O vain man, that faith without works is dead?

True faith in Christ, which is salvation, cannot be kept within. It will spring forth in action because it engenders love. One could go around the world doing good works and not be saved. One must look at the reason and origin of the acts. The works may seem good to us but they do not arise from a heart of love and are not of God. A saved man, who would have the love of God in him, could not live without loving. Faith in God brings forth salvation and God in us. God in us brings forth love and love will bring forth action and works of love, compassion, mercy, and charity.

MAT 7:18 A good tree cannot bring forth evil fruit, neither can a corrupt tree bring forth good fruit. 19 Every tree that bringeth not forth good fruit is hewn down, and cast into the fire. 20 Wherefore by their fruits ye shall know them.

EPH 5:9 (For the fruit of the Spirit is in all goodness and righteousness and truth;) 10 Proving what is acceptable unto the Lord.

GAL 5:22 But the fruit of the Spirit is love, joy, peace, longsuffering, gentleness, goodness, faith, 23 Meekness, temperance: against such there is no law.   24 And they that are Christ's have crucified the flesh with the affections and lusts. 25 If we live in the Spirit, let us also walk in the Spirit.

OF FLESH, LAW, AND MAN

Christianity is a direct connection between God and man, and thus must be viewed in this context continually. Man was made for God by God and as such, the fleshly clothing of the body cannot be in enmity with God. For how could Christ offer up to God anything corrupt? He could not. So if Christ, having been born in the flesh, offered up to God his body as a sacrifice, it becomes obvious the nature of flesh is not corrupt. Unlike the Gnostic and Eastern religions, Christianity does not seek to be free of the fleshy clothing of the body in order to be glorified; instead we seek to be clothed thrice, first in this body, then with the glory of God as He would allow His spirit to reside with us in this earthly tent, and finally with a heavenly garment given us by Christ as we are changed to be like Him when we shall see Him.

1JO 3:2 Beloved, now are we the sons of God, and it doth not yet appear what we shall be: but we know that, when he shall appear, we shall be like him; for we shall see him as he is.

The body is not a prison to be endured but a vehicle by which God may be worshiped and praised. Indeed, the flesh, being the same in kind as that of Christ himself, is the temple of the Holy Spirit and is the way through which God now chooses to announce His plan of salvation as it is written:

ROM 10:13 For whosoever shall call upon the name of the Lord shall be saved. How then shall they call on him in whom they have not believed? and how shall they believe in him of whom they have not heard? and how shall they hear without a preacher? 15 And how shall they preach, except they be sent? as it is written, How beautiful are the feet of them that preach the gospel of peace, and bring glad tidings of good things!

23

It is therefore not the flesh, which wars against God, but the law of carnality that the flesh obeys. As it has been from his creation, man has obeyed this carnal law and has, through his mortal weakness, turned away from the higher law, which is a spiritual law.

ROM 7:22 For I delight in the law of God after the inward man: 23 But I see another law in my members, warring against the law of my mind, and bringing me into captivity to the law of sin which is in my members.

Still, man was commanded to follow God's laws and could not do so. Even as we agreed that the law was good, even as we could hear God's will speaking to us through the law, even as we adopted the law as our mandate, we failed to keep the law. Not one man in thousands of years and millions of lifetimes, or for that matter in the whole of humanity, could fulfill the law. How then could God be called a good and faithful judge when it was not possible to keep His commandments? What wise judge would give a man an impossible task and then demand his life when it could not be done? But one man has kept the law and by doing so both condemned us and saved us. Condemnation did not come from Him but in the fact the law was kept and fulfilled by Him. Man was shown it was possible to keep the law and was thus condemned by the law having no excuses left. Yet, in the complete and perfect fulfillment of the law, Christ was blameless and in this state He died to impart to us His perfection, having laid down His life for this purpose, to pay for our sins with His perfect life, trading sin for death as it is written, "The wages of sin is death".

When we were deceived by sin to think the fulfillment of our desires would bring us life, or at least a richer life, we became the slave of sin, led away by our own greed as surely as any sailor was seduced and shanghaied into slavery. Unable to see the fruits of our decision, we stumble forward as children, blind to the consequences of our actions. As mutual trust of friends or spouses is broken by a single lie, so sin enters in by a single act, neither path having been conceived by the liar or sinner until consequences destroy him. Thus, in trying to bring about a better life, we bring forth death which is the payment meted out by our master to us. In spite of our actions and consequences, following Christ fulfilled the law for us. We who are incapable of doing so would be saved by the law itself through an act of grace, in which an innocent life was offered up freely for those who were not innocent. Even though our bodies still war against us to obey the laws of carnality our spirit lives in Christ and through Christ because of His righteousness.

MAT 5:17 Think not that I am come to destroy the law, or the prophets: I am not come to destroy, but to fulfil. 18 For verily I say unto you, Till heaven and earth pass, one jot or one tittle shall in no wise pass from the law, till all be fulfilled.

The lowest carnality, which is pride and is the primal sin, is seen in the desire to "be good" as the law gives zeal to the unenlightened man.

PRO 13:10 Only by pride cometh contention: but with the well advised is wisdom.

PRO 16:18 Pride goeth before destruction, and an haughty spirit before a fall.

1JO 2:16 For all that is in the world, the lust of the flesh, and the lust of the eyes, and the pride of life, is not of the Father, but is of the world.

PHI 3:4 Though I might also have confidence in the flesh. If any other man thinketh that he hath whereof he might trust in the flesh, I more: 5 Circumcised the eighth day, of the stock of Israel, of the tribe of Benjamin, an Hebrew of the Hebrews; as touching the law, a Pharisee; 6 Concerning zeal, persecuting the church; touching the righteousness which is in the law, blameless. 7 But what things were gain to me, those I counted loss for Christ. 8 Yea doubtless, and I count all things but loss for the excellency of the knowledge of Christ Jesus my Lord: for whom I have suffered the loss of all things, and do count them but dung, that I may win Christ, 9 And be found in him, not having mine

25

own righteousness, which is of the law, but that which is through the faith of Christ, the righteousness which is of God by faith:

In pursuit of the letter of the law the foundation and reason of the law is lost beneath man's self-righteousness. The foundation and reason of the law was always love. Love of God and love of one's fellow man is the whole of all law, as stated by Christ. It is also the only thing we cannot "do", since these are internal and attitudinal things springing from one's nature and not one's actions. How could our nature be changed?   Man was given the law by God to force this question to be asked. God becomes the only answer due to man's inadequacies to change his own nature.

Instead of embracing this knowledge and admitting dependence on God, man turns a blind and prideful eye to the only law that matters and focuses on those items of action he can hope to obey. We tithe, go to church, pray before meals, work in the church, and dress according to church standards. We know all of the answers in Sunday school, exhibit a never fading smile, and can defend and explain our theology, but we do not have love in our hearts and the Spirit of the living God is not resident in us. This is form without substance; answers without understanding. It is modern Phariseeism.

1CO 13:3 And though I bestow all my goods to feed the poor, and though I give my body to be burned, and have not charity, it profiteth me nothing.

Spiritual pride is the most common form of sin in the church. It is all-pervasive and is a direct indication of the flesh rearing its ugly head as we insist action and law count more than grace and love. Men may be blind, but God is not. The spirit of the law, which is faith, humility, and love, will be judged as righteousness. So flesh, in an attempt to "do" and "act" zealously toward the keeping of the law, plunges man headlong into condemnation thinking, in his pride, man could keep that which is perfect. Man convinces himself of this but ignoring those areas he cannot control, such as his own heart, he focuses instead on an outward show of law and duty. But the law was made to show man his shortcomings and thus draw him back to Him who is perfect, the maker and keeper of the law.

LUK 18:11 The Pharisee stood and prayed thus with himself, God, I thank thee, that I am not as other men are, extortioners, unjust, adulterers, or even as this publican. 12 I fast twice in the week, I give tithes of all that I possess. 13 And the publican, standing afar off, would not lift up so much as his eyes unto heaven, but smote upon his breast, saying, God be merciful to me a sinner. 14 I tell you, this man went down to his house justified rather than the other: for every one that exalteth himself shall be abased; and he that humbleth himself shall be exalted.

It was pride in the angelic host that was the cause and root of sin. It was pride that was propagated into man and caused the downfall. It is pride that controls and blinds us.

ISA 14:11 Thy pomp is brought down to the grave, and the noise of thy viols: the worm is spread under thee, and the worms cover thee.12 How art thou fallen from heaven, O Lucifer, son of the morning! how art thou cut down to the ground, which didst weaken the nations!

GEN 2:25 And they were both naked, the man and his wife, and were not ashamed.3:1 Now the serpent was more subtle than any beast of the field which the LORD God had made. And he said unto the woman, Yea, hath God said, Ye shall not eat of every tree of the garden? 2 And the woman said unto the serpent, We may eat of the fruit of the trees of the garden: 3 But of the fruit of the tree which is in the midst of the garden, God hath said, Ye shall not eat of it, neither shall ye touch it, lest ye die. 4 And the serpent said unto the woman, Ye shall not surely die: 5 For God doth know that in the day ye eat thereof, then your eyes shall be opened, and ye shall be as gods, knowing good and evil. 6 And when the woman saw that the tree was good for food, and that it was pleasant to the eyes, and a tree to be desired to make one wise, she took of the fruit thereof, and did eat, and gave also unto her husband with her; and he did eat.

It continues to be pride that keeps us from seeing the truth of our own nature and existence. Pride and arrogance are grouped together with evil, although we may think evil is on a different and lower level, closer to Satan himself. These four, pride, arrogance, insolence, and evil arise from the same root and are manifestations of the same, all too common, human condition.

PRO 8:13 The fear of the LORD is to hate evil: pride, and arrogancy, and the evil way, and the forward mouth, do I hate.

The root and cause of all four arise from a self-centered viewpoint that takes no one else into consideration. They come from tunnel vision so narrow as to include only the person and his desires. This calls into question the nature of evil. Does evil have a reasoned intent to hurt, kill, and destroy or is there an egomaniacal innocence to evil? Could it be that complete evil is actually a blind selfishness? It is not that the evil man does not make evil plans, he does, but he seldom if ever takes his consequences or the feelings of others into consideration. Only his feelings matter to him. His thoughts and actions are based on fulfilling his own desires at the expense of all others. Feelings and welfare of others do not come into play, nor do they cross his mind. The nature of evil is a twisted, childish, innocent, self-centeredness. How strange and paradoxical; how appropriate Satan should take what was so much a part of him and then assist man in finding it in himself.

ISA 14:12 How art thou fallen from heaven, O Lucifer, son of the morning! how art thou cut down to the ground, which didst weaken the nations! 13 For thou hast said in thine heart, I will ascend into heaven, I will exalt my throne above the stars of God: I will sit also upon the mount of the congregation, in the sides of the north: 14 I will ascend above the heights of the clouds; I will be like the most High.

Truth, love, and mercy are found on the path to God. Putting others before oneself, feeling with and for others, seeking the will of God over our own, this is the path to God and to truth. Compassion and love give way to mercy and mercy is the essence of grace.

PSA 100:3 Know ye that the LORD he is God: it is he that hath made us, and not we ourselves; we are his people, and the sheep of his pasture. 4 Enter into his gates with thanksgiving, and into his courts with praise: be thankful unto him, and bless his name. 5 For the LORD is good; his mercy is everlasting; and his truth endureth to all generations.

PSA 25:10 All the paths of the LORD are mercy and truth unto such as keep his covenant and his testimonies. 11 For thy name's sake, O LORD, pardon mine iniquity; for it is great. 12 What man is he that feareth the LORD? him shall he teach in the way that he shall choose. 13 His soul shall dwell at ease; and his seed shall inherit the earth.

PSA 26:3 For thy loving kindness is before mine eyes: and I have walked in thy truth. 4 I have not sat with vain persons, neither will I go in with dissemblers.   5 I have hated the congregation of evildoers; and will not sit with the wicked.

PSA 31:5 Into thine hand I commit my spirit: thou hast redeemed me, O LORD God of truth.

PSA 85:10 Mercy and truth are met together; righteousness and peace have kissed each other. 11 Truth shall spring out of the earth; and righteousness shall look down from heaven.

PSA 100:5 For the LORD is good; his mercy is everlasting; and his truth endureth to all generations. 101:1 I will sing of mercy and judgment: unto thee, O LORD, will I sing.

What is the truth? Jesus Christ is truth.

JOH 1:14 And the Word was made flesh, and dwelt among us, (and we beheld his glory, the glory as of the only begotten of the Father,) full of grace and truth.

TRANSITIONS OF LOVE

"If I could just see him", I said, "I know I could have faith." "If I could only look into His eyes, I know I would love Him with all my heart." "If I could hear His sweet voice I would be His forever." So weak is the heart that we play these games of excuses with ourselves, explaining why we waiver in our faith or feeling. But, these excuses are worthless.

Three years they were together. Peter had seen Jesus almost every day for three years. He had seen Him walk on water. He had seen Him die and now Jesus sat in front of Peter talking to Him. The conversation was simple, but the Lord's words were carefully chosen. They cut to the point in one question. Before we explore the conversation we must hearken back to the meaning of the word "Agape'". Remember it is an unconditional love full of grace and completeness.

Agape' is the word for Godly love. It is charity, selfless love, giving without expectation. To love with one's whole heart unselfishly.

This is quite different from the other word for love used between them.

"Philo" is a brotherly love. It is fondness, friendship, and family type of love.

Let us look closely at the conversation between Peter and Jesus. Notice the root words of Philo and Agape' within the words chosen by each, Jesus and Peter.

JOH 21:14 This is now the third time that Jesus shewed himself to his disciples, after that he was risen from the dead. 15 So when they had dined, Jesus saith to Simon Peter, Simon, son of Jonas, lovest (agapas) thou me more than these? He saith unto him, Yea, Lord; thou knowest that I love (philo) thee. He saith unto him, Feed my lambs. 16 He saith to him again the second time, Simon, son of Jonas, lovest (agapas) thou me? He saith unto him, Yea, Lord; thou knowest that I love (philo)

31

thee. He saith unto him, Feed my sheep. 17 He saith unto him the third time, Simon, son of Jonas, lovest (philis) thou me? Peter was grieved because he said unto him the third time, Lovest (philo) thou me? And he said unto him, Lord, thou knowest all things; thou knowest that I love (philo) thee. Jesus saith unto him, Feed my sheep.

Concentrating on the questions and answers only, the conversation takes on a startling contrast. Peter was attempting to answer the question to Jesus' satisfaction without lying, but his heart betrayed him.

Simon Peter, do you love me with all your heart?

Lord, you know I love you like a brother.

Simon, son of Jonas, do you love me with all your heart?

Lord, you know I love you like a brother.

Simon Peter, son of Jonas, do you love me like a brother?

Yes, Lord, you know I love you like a brother.

Peter, having lived with God, seen Him die for his sins, and now looking into the face of the resurrected Lord, can only admit fondness. What fools we are to think we could do better. But there is hope! The comforter, the Holy Spirit descended at Pentecost and the church was born, but so were the hearts of man. Now able to live and move and have our being with the Spirit of the living God within us, our hearts are converted.

1PE 1:7 That the trial of your faith, being much more precious than of gold that perisheth, though it be tried with fire, might be found unto praise and honour and glory at the appearing of Jesus Christ:

8 Whom having not seen, ye love (agapate'); in whom, though now ye see him not, yet believing, ye rejoice with joy unspeakable and full of glory: 9 Receiving the end of your faith, even the salvation of your souls.

1PE 4:8 And above all things have fervent charity (agapin) among yourselves: for charity (agapin) shall cover the multitude of sins.

Peter, being changed through the power of the spirit of God living within him, was brought to a state of love so deep and profound that at the time of his death he requested to be crucified upside-down, not being worthy to even die as Jesus died. Such a glorious change will happen to us also, not being contingent upon seeing Him except in spirit. The changed is forged by His spirit in us.

A PEOPLE IN ERROR

Why are you proud, dust and ashes? The Tree of Life by St. Bonaventure

Any relationship based on an exchange of tangibles is only as stable as the desire or supply of the tangibles. This includes salvation, heaven, and glory. It is in this simple statement the failure of "mundane" Christianity rests.

Devotion based on threat becomes servitude. The devotee situated as an ox between the carrot of heaven and the goad of hell is bound to fail just as the ox will tire and fall. But, devotion springing from a heart of love is not indenturement, but service, not blackmail but charity. It is not in seeking the rewards of Christ but in seeking the heart of Christ we find the answer. We must love without motive, and not let this aim itself become a motive. Love must spring from a pure heart. Even seeking a pure heart is a motive, which defeats the purpose of God flowing through us unimpeded by us. To approach the heart of God is to have God bring us to Him. Thus, we do nothing but become beggars, waiting for an act of grace. Rules, doctrine, heaven, and hell do not matter. Church law and opinion become dung. Our hearts cry out for the beloved. Only He matters. It is only Him we seek.

Each year the church loses thousands of souls. Men and women give up, become discouraged and turn their backs on the church. They become apostate all because of false expectations and teachings. Many understand the true path at the time of conversion. They experience the heart of God and are joyous in it, but soon they are drawn away from God and are made to listen to doctrine and church laws which have nothing to do with what they are experiencing. Soon the flame dies as one living too long away from the beloved. They desire to return to the beloved but the church can no longer show them the way, only continue to preach moral lessons and church doctrine, which are as devoid of the life of God as the dried bones of a man's corpse.

34

This thing called Christianity is a heart condition. It is a relationship. It is a love affair. It is a mystical and circular relationship of "bringing forth". These are the three comings of Christ: His incarnation at the crowning of creation, the second coming when we invite Him into our hearts, and the third coming is when He comes in glory at the end of the age. God created man and then became man. Man submits to God and through God's salvation man brings forth the spirit of God into this world where it is shared with others. In time, those with whom we share will also welcome into themselves the Spirit of God where there will be love and communion and birth of the spirit of Christ on earth through them. What could be more intimate than to be made by God and have God birthed in you? What could be more personal than the same vows of marriage to love, honor, and obey said to a Holy and sacred spouse? He is a spouse who knows us because He made us. He knows us because we live in Him. He knows us because He lives within us.

We cannot know God through doctrine, although doctrine attempts in someway to describe, qualify, and quantify God's laws. This approach is much like using the laws in our legal system to describe our lifestyle of personal freedom here in the United States. The confusion arises from the use of the word "know". There are different levels or ways to "know". One can know about something or someone by reading a book. This is knowledge without application. One can know something or someone by experiencing it or them. In the experiencing of the thing there is a depth and understanding which comes with being in relationship with the person or thing.

Scripture gives us information and knowledge about God. It does not give us the experience of God, nor does Scripture give us a relationship with God. If it did then anyone who read the Bible would be saved. Doctrines are rules and laws derived from the interpretation of Scripture or assigned as a rule by a body governing a denomination. Doctrine comes about for two main reasons; to defend against a heresy, and to describe a difference between theological ideas. In the early days of the church, doctrine was used primarily to defend against ideas the founding fathers saw as antithetical to Christianity. Indeed, much of the New Testament is made up of letters written in part to state and establish doctrine in order to correct error in the church. These are necessary to those who do not understand the idea of Christianity, thinking it is a religion and set of beliefs, or a group of people to be led. Christ himself reduced all doctrine to two phrases.

MAT 22:36 Master, which is the great commandment in the law? 37 Jesus said unto him, Thou shalt love the Lord thy God with all thy heart, and with all thy soul, and with all thy mind. 38 This is the first and great commandment. 39 And the second is like unto it, Thou shalt love thy neighbour as thyself. 40 On these two commandments hang all the law and the prophets. "

The meaning and implications are obvious. If we have the proper relationship with God and our fellow man we would not sin.

This is, on the surface, too much to ask of our sinful nature. It does, however, show us the exact place doctrine plays, or should play, in our Christian lives. Even in knowing what is right and wrong, we choose to do what relieves our desires. Knowing the rules, laws, or doctrine does no good since it is beyond our power to do what is right. If we were capable of following the laws of God, Christ would not have had to come. He would have come anyway so He might crown humanity with His glory, for Christ is the crown of humanity. It is only in submitting to God and being remade by Him do we have any hope of overcoming our own primal nature.

The other use of doctrine today is to establish a framework of beliefs, which are used to distinguish one denomination from another. Most of us do not even know what our own denominations proclaim as doctrine. In the church which I attend, we have a wonderful Sunday school class and lively discussions ensue. Many of us were talking about the "priesthood of the believer". This is a concept that holds there is no difference between the ability of a priest or a layperson who is a Christian to approach God, pray, anoint, give communion, or lay on hands since the full price of sacrifice had been paid for all believers.

All agreed that anyone who belonged to Christ was a child of God and could ask the Father for any of these things. "Why it is then that the Book of Discipline tells us the only one who can bless the host is an ordained minister of this denomination?" After a moment of stunned silence I was asked to "show them in the book". I did so and the response was, "Well, no one believes everything that their denomination believes." That much is true. Denominations spring up as a result of the narrow-minded and tunnel vision tendencies of humankind. An idea or theological point is seized upon, usually to the exclusion of other balancing points. As it was with the views of predestination and foreknowledge, both of which have points and counterpoints in scripture, the full truth will not be known and cannot be comprehended until such time as our finite minds are made infinitely perfect.

Yet, these are but two of the divisive views over which stubborn people fight and part fellowship, all in the name of knowing God better. If we were to do away with such trivial notions and rest in His perfect mind we would find how much we cannot know and how little difference it makes to the final destination of loving Him. For Christians, not the religious, not the churchgoers, but for those who actively seek His heart and not His rules; doctrine, church tradition and laws serve little purpose at all. Many times it is a limitation and hindrance to the journey of reaching toward Him. Do we love God? Do we love the brethren? Let us go on from here.

Doctrine is like glass, you can see the truth through it but it separates you from the truth. Scripture is not God. Church tradition is not God. They are only reflections and pictures of Him. It is not that doctrine and scripture are of no use. They are very useful. They serve as measuring rods by which we may see our shortcomings and inadequacies. They serve as a schoolmaster and guide us so we do not diverge into heresy.

2TI 3:15 And that from a child thou hast known the holy scriptures, which are able to make thee wise unto salvation through faith which is in Christ Jesus. 16 All scripture is given by inspiration of

37

God, and is profitable for doctrine, for reproof, for correction, for instruction in righteousness: 17
That the man of God may be perfect, throughly furnished unto all good works.

We may learn of Him through doctrine but that is not the same as knowing Him.

Only in a living, growing relationship can we EXPERIENCE God. This is the only way to KNOW Him. We must now go beyond doctrine into His heart so that we may form a relationship with Him. Doctrine and law become of no consequence when we are obedient to the one who is the source of righteousness.   How can we go against God's law when we are obedient to and guided by the Spirit of God? Yet, should we say we would not sin? Our imperfect and unstable gaze would betray us. But the work of God in us will be seen as we revisit our sins less and less often over longer and longer intervals as He remakes us into His image. The use of doctrine should be limited to assuring we do not stray from this path.

It is because of man's unsteady and skewed gaze that the curse of denominations arose. The very idea that we could see God's entire picture at once, clearly, and in balance speaks to the egotism of man. Denomination can be defined as a focus or obsession on an idea or set of ideas to the point of the imbalance of the whole. Whether it is baptism by water, the faithfulness of God in the face of our faithlessness, the power of the clergy over the members, divorce, works verses grace, predestination verses foreknowledge, who can give communion, or the number of days the baptismal water should be kept, a church may split or denomination may arise over the dispute.   Within the church, all denominations arose out of disputation over points of political control, doctrine, or interpretation of scripture, most of which are vain and meaningless. None of which would have happened if the love of God had overcome the love of selfish pride and the search for power.

To keep this kind of conflict from happening in our own hearts, let us put Christ first. Our theology will become simple and God centered as we turn away from the wisdom and opinions of man. Let us do as Paul said, "For I determined not to know any thing among you, save Jesus Christ, and him crucified. And I was with you in weakness, and in fear, and in much trembling. And my speech and my preaching was not with enticing words of man's wisdom, but in demonstration of the Spirit and of power: That your faith should not stand in the wisdom of men, but in the power of God." 1CO 2:2 –5

HEB 5:13 For every one that useth milk is unskillful in the word of righteousness: for he is a babe. 14 But strong meat belongeth to them that are of full age, even those who by reason of use have their senses exercised to discern both good and evil. 6:1 Therefore leaving the principles of the doctrine of Christ, let us go on unto perfection; not laying again the foundation of repentance from dead works, and of faith toward God, 2 Of the doctrine of baptisms, and of laying on of hands, and of resurrection of the dead, and of eternal judgment.   3 And this will we do, if God permit.

This "perfection" (maturing) we seek is beyond the basic principles we have studied all of our lives. What we seek does not abide in words but in the act of loving Him. We must now put learning into action.

1JO 3:13 Marvel not, my brethren, if the world hate you. 14 We know that we have passed from death unto life, because we love the brethren. He that loveth not his brother abideth in death. ...16 Hereby perceive we the love of God, because he laid down his life for us: and we ought to lay down our lives for the brethren....18 My little children, let us not love in word, neither in tongue; but in deed and in truth.

ACTS 17:27 That they should seek the Lord, if haply they might feel after him, and find him, though he be not far from every one of us: 28 For in him we live, and move, and have our being; as certain also of your own poets have said, For we are also his offspring.

JOH 17:19 And for their sakes I sanctify myself, that they also might be sanctified through the truth. 20 Neither pray I for these alone, but for them also which shall believe on me through their word; 21 That they all may be one; as thou, Father, art in me, and I in thee, that they also may be one in us: that the world may believe that thou hast sent me. 22 And the glory which thou gavest me I have given them; that they may be one, even as we are one: 23 I in them, and thou in me, that they may be made perfect in one; and that the world may know that thou hast sent me, and hast loved them, as thou hast loved me.

ROM 8:9 But ye are not in the flesh, but in the Spirit, if so be that the Spirit of God dwell in you. Now if any man have not the Spirit of Christ, he is none of his. 10 And if Christ be in you, the body is dead because of sin; but the Spirit is life because of righteousness. 11 But if the Spirit of him that raised up Jesus from the dead dwell in you, he that raised up Christ from the dead shall also quicken your mortal bodies by his Spirit that dwelleth in you.

We have become justified by our faith in Jesus Christ, yet we still measure ourselves against the law. Salvation is not quid pro quo. We can never live up to the law. Why do we still strive to keep the law? If we keep the law because we believe it assures our salvation we are wrong. For all have sinned and fallen short, all have failed to keep the law, and all were doomed to die in sin. Then grace came to us all.

Christians seek to do the law. Most Christians still live as if they were under the law. Most struggle daily to do what God has said is impossible to do. They become fatigued, defeated, or self-righteous in their struggle. Some become proud of their accomplishments in keeping the law. They convince themselves they have somehow come up to God's standards and are justified by their actions. None are good but God. These have not plumbed the depths of their lying and deceiving hearts. Most people realize the impossibility of fulfilling the law. They become beaten down by their own sin.

Yet, we are released from our sin through faith. Many lean to their memories of what they have accomplished for God. Preachers, pastors, and Sunday school teachers point to time and effort spent in ministry as if there were some payment with which to recompense God. It is like trading rags for gold. God will not allow us to settle on our lees. (In the making of wine the winemaker would pour the wine though cloth in order to strain it of the lees or sediment. The sediment or lees that was left would settle to the bottom of the jar. He would then pour off the clarified wine into another vessel and repeat the process again until the wine was pure. If the lees were to settle and the wine not be purified it would spoil and become rancid.) This is not to better our standing before God, but to better our state of being.

The error in understanding comes from the confusion between our "STATE" and our "STANDING". Our standing before God is one of righteousness. Our state is that of a wretched man. We stand blameless before God because Christ Jesus has fulfilled the law for us and died for us as the breaking of the law required from us. He released us from the law and any debt we have owed and would owe the law. Our state as human beings has not changed. We are still wretched sinners. It is our flesh and sinful nature, warring against the spirit, which causes our state to be different from our standing. These two, state and standing, cannot be confused. Jesus gives us our standing before God once and for all through His death on the cross. Our state is changed slowly as we are conformed into His image as the Spirit lives within us. We may work to better our state so that God may be more easily seen in us and that He may be glorified in the eyes of others.

MAT 5:16 Let your light so shine before men, that they may see your good works, and glorify your Father which is in heaven.

Do not think for one moment you can add a single atom to the work done by Christ to establish our standing before God. We have no need for law. Christ was the end of the law for us. If God is in us and we are in Him then the law has turned to love. We can be free to love and do what we will if the

41

spirit of God guides us. Yet, being unstable creatures with deceptive hearts, we need the Holy Scriptures in order to check ourselves and avoid straying into error. We should not seek to be free of the law, nor should we seek to be bound by the law. We should go beyond this trap of law and seek only God and His will.

Our State is bound in Christ's death and God's forgiveness.

JOB 14:16   For now thou numberest my steps: dost thou not watch over my sin? 17   My transgression is sealed up in a bag, and thou sewest up mine iniquity.

EPH 1:10 That in the dispensation of the fullness of times he might gather together in one all things in Christ, both which are in heaven, and which are on earth; even in him: 11 In whom also we have obtained an inheritance, being predestinated according to the purpose of him who worketh all things after the counsel of his own will: 12 That we should be to the praise of his glory, who first trusted in Christ. 13 In whom ye also trusted, after that ye heard the word of truth, the gospel of your salvation: in whom also after that ye believed, ye were sealed with that Holy Spirit of promise, 14 Which is the earnest of our inheritance until the redemption of the purchased possession, unto the praise of his glory.

1JO 2:1 My little children, these things write I unto you, that ye sin not. And if any man sin, we have an advocate with the Father, Jesus Christ the righteous: 2 And he is the propitiation for our sins: and not for ours only, but also for the sins of the whole world.

In this dual existence of standing and state, man is kept safe from himself and his sinful nature he cannot control. Jesus keeps us as His own, having bought us with His life. We are His. The price for breaking God's spiritual laws was paid. The fine was collected and the punishment meted out. Jesus paid it all and took the punishment for us. Our standing with God, our judge, is good once again and we are counted as righteous. Yet, the state of man at the point of salvation has not changed. He is the same in the natural or carnal sense as he was the moment before. From this point on the state of man will be altered by the spirit working in him and by his obedience to the spirit. It may happen in leaps of epiphany as he sees his errors and sinful ways or it may happen in long periods of maturing as God works to mold us into His image. This is not to say instantaneous healing does not occur. It certainly does, but it does not happen all the time and is in God's hands. Like epiphanies that remain, healings are not the rule, but through acts of grace, God sheds His love on us as He wills.

Like a sculptor working in stone, the image God wishes to reveal in us is manifest by removing those pieces He does not want in us: pride, arrogance, lust, greed, and all of the other unwanted parts of sinful man. Our state, in time, should become more and more like that of Adam before the fall wherein there is more obedience and friendship to God and less rebelliousness and sin. It may be argued that we have some say so in our state in that we can choose to do God's will or not. We may choose to follow the spirit's leadings or not. In this narrow and inadequate way we are culpable. The culpability only serves to enforce our need for a savior each time we choose to give in to our desires instead of His will.

1CO 6:12 All things are lawful unto me, but all things are not expedient: all things are lawful for me, but I will not be brought under the power of any.   13 Meats for the belly, and the belly for meats: but God shall destroy both it and them. Now the body is not for fornication, but for the Lord; and the Lord for the body. 14 And God hath both raised up the Lord, and will also raise up us by his own power. 15 Know ye not that your bodies are the members of Christ? shall I then take the members of Christ, and make them the members of a harlot? God forbid. 16 What? know ye not that he which is joined to a harlot is one body? for two, saith he, shall be one flesh. 17 But he that is joined unto the Lord is one spirit.

I am not preaching freedom from God, only freedom from the law. I am not preaching freedom to sin, but freedom from sin. If we believe Jesus saved us and wishes to husband our spirit, why then do we seek to lord over our own actions and thoughts? We cannot be holy. We cannot keep ourselves from sin. He must move in us to do these things. Thus, our energies should be spent in listening to Him and being guided by Him, not in seeking to keep ourselves under some private spiritual law. In our yielding to Him, we become servant and spouse to Him.

JOH 1:17 For the law was given by Moses, but grace and truth came by Jesus Christ.

ROM 2:11 For there is no respect of persons with God. 12 For as many as have sinned without law shall also perish without law: and as many as have sinned in the law shall be judged by the law; 13 For not the hearers of the law are just before God, but the doers of the law shall be justified. 14 For when the Gentiles, which have not the law, do by nature the things contained in the law, these, having not the law, are a law unto themselves:15 Which shew the work of the law written in their hearts, their conscience also bearing witness, and their thoughts the meanwhile accusing or else excusing one another; 16 In the day when God shall judge the secrets of men by Jesus Christ according to my gospel.

Righteousness is not the absence of unrighteousness. Just as a good man is not a man who simply does not steal or kill. The absence of evil does not make one good. It leaves one in a state of common conformity and lukewarm social acceptability. There must be an action or actions to bring someone from that which is not bad to that which is good. Man cannot change his state of unrighteousness since only one action can be performed which will bring him into a state of righteousness. This change of state is called justification. The act of justification is possible because of the act of redemption. To redeem something is to buy it. Christ paid our debt to God and thus bought our freedom from sin and its "fines". Christ bought us as one would buy a slave.

ROM 6:14 For sin shall not have dominion over you: for ye are not under the law, but under grace. 15 What then? shall we sin, because we are not under the law, but under grace? God forbid. 16 Know ye not, that to whom ye yield yourselves servants to obey, his servants ye are to whom ye obey; whether of sin unto death, or of obedience unto righteousness? 17 But God be thanked, that ye were the servants of sin, but ye have obeyed from the heart that form of doctrine which was delivered you. 18 Being then made free from sin, ye became the servants of righteousness.

So, we are bought when we accept His payment, His life for our sins. This act of paying for us is redemption. It is acquired through faith in the fact that Christ came in the flesh and died for this purpose. Following on the heels of redemption is justification. Christ is sinless and we, upon being redeemed by faith are also justified by faith being in Christ and therefore justified in Him for He is just and perfect. We are made righteous by being clothed in righteousness because we are clothed in Him. We are justified through faith in Christ, not by man's own righteousness, for there is no deed or deeds man could perform that would make him righteous in the sight of God.

Since sin and unrighteousness are the flowers that spring from the root of man's nature it seems obvious man would not have the power to love God and neighbor with any more consistence than his sinful nature could endure. Certainly, man could not love either more than himself. Knowing man cannot fulfill the inner law of love, God has created a path through which man can be redeemed by the love of another who has perfect love. It is Christ. He is our atonement, our redeemer, our justifier, our reconciler, our Lord, our King, our God. Man is reconciled to God once again and for the final time.

ROM 3:20 Therefore by the deeds of the law there shall no flesh be justified in his sight: for by the law is the knowledge of sin. 21 But now the righteousness of God without the law is manifested, being witnessed by the law and the prophets; 22 Even the righteousness of God which is by faith of Jesus Christ unto all and upon all them that believe: for there is no difference: 23 For all have

45

sinned, and come short of the glory of God; 24 Being justified freely by his grace through the redemption that is in Christ Jesus:

ROM 3:28 Therefore we conclude that a man is justified by faith without the deeds of the law.

ROM 6:14 For sin shall not have dominion over you: for ye are not under the law, but under grace. 15 What then? shall we sin, because we are not under the law, but under grace? God forbid. 16 Know ye not, that to whom ye yield yourselves servants to obey, his servants ye are to whom ye obey; whether of sin unto death, or of obedience unto righteousness? 17 But God be thanked, that ye were the servants of sin, but ye have obeyed from the heart that form of doctrine which was delivered you. Being then made free from sin, ye became the servants of righteousness.

ROM 10:4 For Christ is the end of the law for righteousness to every one that believeth.

ROM 13:10 Love worketh no ill to his neighbour: therefore love is the fulfilling of the law.

1CO 15:55 O death, where is thy sting? O grave, where is thy victory? 56 The sting of death is sin; and the strength of sin is the law. 57 But thanks be to God, which giveth us the victory through our Lord Jesus Christ.

GAL 2:16 Knowing that a man is not justified by the works of the law, but by the faith of Jesus Christ, even we have believed in Jesus Christ, that we might be justified by the faith of Christ, and not by the works of the law: for by the works of the law shall no flesh be justified.

GAL 5:2 Behold, I Paul say unto you, that if ye be circumcised, Christ shall profit you nothing. 3 For I testify again to every man that is circumcised, that he is a debtor to do the whole law. 4 Christ is become of no effect unto you, whosoever of you are justified by the law; ye are fallen from grace. 5

For we through the Spirit wait for the hope of righteousness by faith. 6 For in Jesus Christ neither circumcision availeth any thing, nor uncircumcision; but faith which worketh by love.

ROM 3:23 For all have sinned, and come short of the glory of God; 24 Being justified freely by his grace through the redemption that is in Christ Jesus: 25 Whom God hath set forth to be a propitiation through faith in his blood, to declare his righteousness for the remission of sins that are past, through the forbearance of God; 26 To declare, I say, at this time his righteousness: that he might be just, and the justifier of him which believeth in Jesus. 27 Where is boasting then? It is excluded. By what law? of works? Nay: but by the law of faith. 28 Therefore we conclude that a man is justified by faith without the deeds of the law.

DESIRE, SIN, and EVIL

The Mystery of Sin

It seems fundamentally axiomatic that a creature cannot supercede its creator. After all, if one creates something one should be able to control that thing which is created. God created man and is obviously above him. Then man with his carnal nature created sin. Yet, now man is controlled by sin. One may say man is a slave to sin. This is a great mystery. The mystery of sin is that somehow the creation has become lord over the creator. Never before and never since in the history of creation has this happened. Only God himself who created man can set this straight. Only in God, the creator of all things, can the great mystery of sin be solved. He who created all things can save man from all things.

One may argue that sin was created before man through the actions of Satan. This would be true of a spiritual plan where angels tread and demons fall. One may say if God created all things then God also created sin. In this case I would like to use a mundane example and simply say God created man who created the shirt I am wearing. The shirt is made by man but man was made by God. One may say the decisions of man simply allowed sin into mankind. But on a much more individual level and a level concerning mankind itself, sin was created for mankind by man. In a way we all create sin in ourselves and in our world by our actions, thoughts, and decisions. Whether sin is created personally or unleashed personally at the point it is manifest it is out of man's control.

Sin demands payment in the form of the life of the person who sinned. Once we have sinned we are dead. Once we are spiritually dead we have no control over spiritual matters such as the revocation of sin. More like a bomb than any other creations, the destruction cannot be recalled. In the carnage of an exploded bomb, even though man created it, he cannot destroy its destruction. Any hope is up to redeemer to pay the price and recover our loss that we may be in control again of our spiritual

48

destinies. The great mystery of sin is that it is the only thing created that controls the one who creates it.

1CO 15:21 For since by man came death, by man came also the resurrection of the dead. 22 For as in Adam all die, even so in Christ shall all be made alive.23 But every man in his own order: Christ the first fruits; afterward they that are Christ's at his coming. 1CO 15:45 And so it is written, The first man Adam was made a living soul; the last Adam was made a quickening spirit. 46 How be it that was not first which is spiritual, but that which is natural; and afterward that which is spiritual. 47 The first man is of the earth, earthy; the second man is the Lord from heaven.

There is within the human heart a tough fibrous root of fallen life whose nature is to possess, always to possess. It covets 'things' with a deep and fierce passion. The pronouns 'my' and 'mine' look innocent enough in print, but their constant and universal use is significant. They express the real nature of the old Adamic man better than a thousand volumes of theology could do... The roots of our hearts have grown down into things, and we dare not pull up one rootlet lest we die. Things have become necessary to us, a development never originally intended. God's gifts now take the place of God, and the whole course of nature is upset by the monstrous substitution.   A. W. Tozer

Souls in deadly sin look to nothing but how they might find nourishment in the earth. Their appetite is insatiable, but they are never satisfied. They are insatiable and insupportable to their very selves. But it is quite fitting that they should be forever restless, because they have set their desire and will on what will give them nothing but emptiness.

...This is why they can never be satisfied: They are always hankering after what is finite. But they are infinite in the sense that they will never cease to be, even

49

though because of their deadly sin they have ceased to be in grace. Catherine of Siena

Desire is a direct result of man's infinitely expanding appetite. Our stomachs, like our carnal souls, stretch to accommodate an ever-growing desire for more, faster, higher, better... Desire gives way to hunger and a starving man is a fool. Foolishness leads us to sin. Sin takes you farther than you want to go, makes you stay longer than you want to stay, and makes you pay more than you want to pay. Of this, I speak with authority, being a sinner, counting myself as a slave kept against my will, drug back at each escape, still in chains but straining daily against them. I await Him who will free me from my captivity once and for all. He is my hope, both in glory and in this present time, Christ Jesus.

No creature is higher than its creator, but all creatures are lower and more base than their creator. God created man and in his animal nature man created sin. Sin, then, is lower than the animals. What have we done? The creature had been given dominion over its creator. Man is lost in a sea of his own making. We await our redemption from this condition. We await Christ Jesus.

ISA 40:31 But they that wait upon the LORD shall renew their strength; they shall mount up with wings as eagles; they shall run, and not be weary; and they shall walk, and not faint. 41:1 Keep silence before me, O islands; and let the people renew their strength: let them come near; then let them speak: let us come near together to judgment.

ROM 7:14 For we know that the law is spiritual: but I am carnal, sold under sin. 15 For that which I do I allow not: for what I would, that do I not; but what I hate, that do I. 16 If then I do that which I would not, I consent unto the law that it is good. 17 Now then it is no more I that do it, but sin that dwelleth in me. 18 For I know that in me (that is, in my flesh,) dwelleth no good thing: for to will is present with me; but how to perform that which is good I find not. 19 For the good that I would I do not: but the evil which I would not, that I do. 20 Now if I do that I would not, it is no more I that do it, but sin that dwelleth in me.

ROM 7:21 I find then a law, that, when I would do good, evil is present with me. 22 For I delight in the law of God after the inward man: 23 But I see another law in my members, warring against the law of my mind, and bringing me into captivity to the law of sin which is in my members. 24 O wretched man that I am! who shall deliver me from the body of this death? 25 I thank God through Jesus Christ our Lord. So then with the mind I myself serve the law of God; but with the flesh the law of sin. 8:1 There is therefore now no condemnation to them which are in Christ Jesus, who walk not after the flesh, but after the Spirit. 2 For the law of the Spirit of life in Christ Jesus hath made me free from the law of sin and death.

For those who are Christians, sin is temporary insanity. Call it disassociation or psychosis of the spirit. We know what we are about to do is wrong, destructive, and in violation of God's law. We know we are likely to fall but onward we rush, headlong into perdition, driven by some silent force, which is part of us but apart from us. Sin is a most malicious schizophrenia. Who can heal my broken mind? Not I, for when I try to heal my broken mind with my broken mind I fall into great confusion and despair. I pressure myself to do what I know is right, and in placing pressure on my troubled mind I widen the pit of torment within me, giving way to that hated weakness. I fall yet again. I dare not move. I cannot even love God as He has commanded without His help. My mind wars against being fixed on Him. In my prayers it runs to and fro into carnal places and refuses rescue. My strength with which I seek to serve the Lord is used up on this rebellious member. I cry out to the Lord for help. I wait for Him who can remake my mind. I seek the MIND OF CHRIST.

MAR 12:30 And thou shalt love the Lord thy God with all thy heart, and with all thy soul, and with all thy mind, and with all thy strength: this is the first commandment.

51

ROM 7:22 For I delight in the law of God after the inward man: 23 But I see another law in my members, warring against the law of my mind, and bringing me into captivity to the law of sin which is in my members. 24 O wretched man that I am! who shall deliver me from the body of this death?

ROM 8:6 For to be carnally minded is death; but to be spiritually minded is life and peace. 7 Because the carnal mind is enmity against God: for it is not subject to the law of God, neither indeed can be.

ROM 12:1 I beseech you therefore, brethren, by the mercies of God, that ye present your bodies a living sacrifice, holy, acceptable unto God, which is your reasonable service. 2 And be not conformed to this world: but be ye transformed by the renewing of your mind, that ye may prove what is that good, and acceptable, and perfect, will of God.

ISA 26:2 Open ye the gates, that the righteous nation which keepeth the truth may enter in. 3 Thou wilt keep him in perfect peace, whose mind is stayed on thee: because he trusteth in thee. 4 Trust ye in the LORD forever: for in the LORD JEHOVAH is everlasting strength:

1CO 2:16 For who hath known the mind of the Lord, that he may instruct him? But we have the mind of Christ. 3:1 And I, brethren, could not speak unto you as unto spiritual, but as unto carnal, even as unto babes in Christ. 2 I have fed you with milk, and not with meat: for hitherto ye were not able to bear it, neither yet now are ye able. 3 For ye are yet carnal: for whereas there is among you envying, and strife, and divisions, are ye not carnal, and walk as men?

PART TWO

KEEPING IT SIMPLE

As we strive for the balance between faith and knowledge, we tend to focus on knowledge or doctrine and what we believe within the world of our faith. It is important to know what we believe as Christians and it is important to be able to articulate and explain it. The point must not be lost, however, that all beliefs, and the doctrine that springs from them, come down to points of faith since even the Bible, its contents, and its inerrancy must be taken on faith. Since in the end all points of Christianity rest on faith, it seems reasonable to keep our points of doctrine simple and seek instead Him who sustains our faith. Not to sound too trite about this, but we should not sweat the small stuff, and most points of doctrine beyond the essentials are small or fine points.

What are the points of concern? What points should we sweat? To find out what the early church fathers, thought we could examine various Christian creeds. These are lists of basic and fundamental beliefs. Each creed was made up of statements of belief. These statements were considered points on which there must be agreement before someone could be accepted into the early church as a Christian. Departure from the basic points of faith was considered a heresy. Although the word "heresy" has taken on a tone we do not like to use today in our permissive society we should consider well the lines we should draw within our own lives beyond which beliefs or actions become unacceptable, lest we also slip into heresy.

The Nicene Creed

53

When the Council of Nicaea **(A.D. 325)** rejected the teaching of Arius, it expressed its position by adopting one of the current Eastern symbols and inserting into it some anti-Arian phrases, resulting in this creed. At the Council of Constantinople **(A.D. 381)** some minor changes were made, and it was reaffirmed at the Council of Chalcedon **(A.D. 451).** It is an essential part of the doctrine and liturgy of the Lutheran churches. Historically it has been used especially at Holy Communion on Sundays and major feasts (except when the Apostles' Creed is used as the Baptismal Creed).

We believe in one God,
the Father, the Almighty,
maker of heaven and earth,
of all that is, seen and unseen.
We believe in one Lord, Jesus Christ,
the only Son of God,
eternally begotten of the Father,
God from God, Light from Light,
true God from true God,
begotten, not made,
of one Being with the Father.
Through Him all things were made.
For us and for our salvation
He came down from heaven;
by the power of the Holy Spirit
He became incarnate from the Virgin Mary, and was made man.
For our sake He was crucified under Pontius Pilate;
He suffered death and was buried.
On the third day He rose again

in accordance with the Scriptures;

He ascended into heaven

and is seated at the right hand of the Father.

He will come again in glory to judge the living and the dead,

and His kingdom will have no end.

We believe in the Holy Spirit, the Lord, the giver of life,

who proceeds from the Father and the Son.

With the Father and the Son He is worshiped and glorified.

He has spoken through the Prophets.

We believe in one holy catholic and apostolic Church.

We acknowledge one baptism for the forgiveness of sins.

We look for the resurrection of the dead,

and the life of the world to come. Amen.

The Old Roman Creed

AS QUOTED BY TERTULLIAN (c. 200)

De Virginibus Velandis	Tertullian	De Praescriptione
Believing in one God Almighty, maker of the world,	We believe one only God,	I believe in one God, maker of the world,
and His Son, Jesus Christ,	and the son of God Jesus Christ,	the Word, called His Son, Jesus Christ,
born of the Virgin Mary,	born of the Virgin,	by the Spirit and power of God the Father made flesh in Mary's womb, and born of her
crucified under Pontius Pilate,	Him suffered died, and buried,	fastened to a cross.
on the third day brought to life from the dead,	Brought back to life,	He rose the third day,

received in heaven,	taken again into heaven,	was caught up into heaven,
sitting now at the right hand of the Father,	sits at the right hand of the Father,	set at the right hand of the Father,
will come to judge the living and the dead	will come to judge the living and the dead	will come with glory to take the good into life eternal, and condemn the wicked to perpetual fire,
	who has sent from the Father the Holy Ghost.	sent the vicarious power of His Holy Spirit,
		to govern believers (In this passage articles 9 and 10 precede 8)
through resurrection of the flesh.		restoration of the flesh.

This table serves to show how incomplete the evidence provided is by mere quotations of the Creed, and how cautiously it must be dealt with. Had we possessed only the "De Virginibus Velandis", we might have said that the article concerning the Holy Ghost did not form part of Tertullian's Creed. Had the "De Virginibus Velandis" been destroyed, we should have declared that Tertullian knew nothing of the clause "suffered under Pontius Pilate". And so forth. While no explicit statement of this composition by the Apostles is forthcoming before the close of the fourth century, earlier Fathers such as Tertullian and St. Irenaeus insist that the "rule of faith" is part of the apostolic tradition. Tertullian in particular in his "De Praescriptione" insists that the rule was instituted by Christ and delivered to us by the apostles.

II. The Old Roman Creed

The Catechism of the Council of Trent apparently assumes the apostolic origin of our existing creed. Pointing to the old Roman form as a template, however that if the old Roman form had been held to be the inspired utterance of the Apostles, it would not have been modified too easily at pleasure of the local churches. In particular, it would never have been entirely supplanted by today's form. Printing them side-by-side best reveals the difference between the two:

Roman	Today
(1) I believe in God the Father Almighty;	(1) I believe in God the Father Almighty *Creator of Heaven and earth*
(2) And in Jesus Christ, His only Son, our Lord;	(2) And in Jesus Christ, His only Son, our Lord;

(3) Who was born of (de) the Holy Ghost and of (ex) the Virgin Mary;	(3) Who was *conceived* by the Holy Ghost, born of the Virgin Mary,
(4) Crucified under Pontius Pilate and buried;	(4) *Suffered* under Pontius Pilate, was crucified, *dead*, and buried;
(5) The third day He rose again from the dead,	(5) *He descended into hell*, the third day He rose again from the dead;
(6) He ascended into Heaven,	(6) He ascended into Heaven, sitteth at the right hand of <u>God</u> the Father *Almighty*;
(7) Sitteth at the right hand of the Father,	(7) From thence He shall come to judge the living and the dead.
(8) Whence He shall come to judge the living and the dead.	(8) *I believe* in the Holy Ghost,
(9) And in the Holy Ghost,	(9) The Holy *Catholic* Church, *the communion of saints*
(10) The Holy Church,	(10) The forgiveness of sins,
(11) The forgiveness of sins;	(11) The resurrection of the body, and
(12) The resurrection of the body.	(12) *life everlasting.*

Please note that the Roman form does not contain the clauses "Creator of heaven and earth", "descended into hell", "the communion of saints", "life everlasting", nor the words "conceived",

58

"suffered", "died", and "Catholic". Many of these additions, but not quite all, were probably known to St. Jerome in Palestine (c. 380.--See Morin in Revue Benedictine, January, 1904) Further additions appear in the creeds of southern Gaul at the beginning of the next century, but Tertullian probably assumed its final shape in Rome itself some time before A.D. 700 (Burn, Introduction, 239; and Journal of Theology Studies, July, 1902). We are not certain as to the reasons leading to the changes, but it could be speculated that they were written as implicit defenses of heresies that were popular throughout the time of the alterations.

The Apostles' Creed

The Apostles' Creed, as we have it now, dates from the eighth century. However, it is a revision of the so-called Old Roman Creed, which was used in the West by the third century. Behind the Old Roman Creed, in turn, were variations, which had roots in the New Testament itself. While this creed does not come from the apostles, its roots are apostolic. It serves as a Baptismal symbol in that it describes the faith into which we are baptized and is used in the rites of Baptism and Affirmation of Baptism.

I believe in God, the Father almighty,
creator of heaven and earth.
I believe in Jesus Christ, His only Son, our Lord.
He was conceived by the power of the Holy Spirit
and born of the Virgin Mary.
He suffered under Pontius Pilate,
was crucified, died, and was buried.
He descended into hell. *
On the third day he rose again.

He ascended into heaven,

and is seated at the right hand of the Father.

He will come again to judge the living and the dead.

I believe in the Holy Spirit,

the holy catholic Church,

the communion of saints,

the forgiveness of sins,

the resurrection of the body,

and the life everlasting. Amen.

*or "He descended to the dead."

Text prepared by the International Consultation on English Texts (ICET) and the English Language Liturgical Consultation (ELLC). Reproduced by permission.

This exposition of the creed was made at the request of Laurentius, a Bishop whose see is unknown, but is conjectured by Fontanini, in his life of Rufinus, to have been Concordia, Rufinus' birthplace. Here is the English translation of the creed, which Rufinus was asked to make commentary on. The date of the writing was about 307 A.D.

I believe in God the Father Almighty, invisible and impassible.   And in Jesus Christ, His only Son, our Lord; Who was born from the Holy Ghost, of the Virgin Mary; Was crucified under Pontius Pilate, and buried; He descended to hell; on the third day He rose again from the dead. He ascended to the heavens; He sitteth at the right hand of the Father; Thence He is to come to judge the quick and the dead. And in the Holy Ghost; The Holy Church. The remission of sins. The resurrection of this flesh.

The Chalcedonian Creed

The Chalcedonian Creed was adopted in the fifth century, at the Council of Chalcedon in 451, which is one of the seven Ecumenical councils accepted by Eastern Orthodox, Catholic, and many Protestant Christian churches.

We, then, following the holy Fathers, all with one consent, teach men to confess one and the same Son, our Lord Jesus Christ, the same perfect in Godhead and also perfect in manhood; truly God and truly man, of a reasonable [rational] soul and body; consubstantial [co-essential] with the Father according to the Godhead, and consubstantial with us according to the Manhood; in all things like unto us, without sin; begotten before all ages of the Father according to the Godhead, and in these latter days, for us and for our salvation, born of the Virgin Mary, the Mother of God, according to the Manhood; one and the same Christ, Son, Lord, only begotten, to be acknowledged in two natures, unconfusedly, unchangeably, indivisibly, inseparably; the distinction of natures being by no means taken away by the union, but rather the property of each nature being preserved, and concurring in one Person and one Subsistence, not parted or divided into two persons, but one and the same Son, and only begotten, God the Word, the Lord Jesus Christ; as the prophets from the beginning [have declared] concerning Him, and the Lord Jesus Christ Himself has taught us, and the Creed of the holy Fathers has handed down to us.

The Athanasian Creed

This creed is of uncertain origin. It was supposedly prepared in the time of Athanasius, the great theologian of the fourth century, although it seems more likely that it dates from the fifth or sixth centuries and is Western in character. It assists the Church in combating two errors that undermined Bible teaching: the denial that God's Son and the Holy Spirit are of one being with the Father; the other a denial that Jesus Christ is true God and true man in one person. It declares that whoever rejects the doctrine of the Trinity and the doctrine of Christ is without the saving faith. Traditionally it is considered the "Trinitarian Creed" and read aloud in corporate worship on Trinity Sunday.

Whoever wants to be saved should above all cling to the catholic faith.

Whoever does not guard it whole and inviolable will doubtless perish eternally.

Now this is the catholic faith: We worship one God in Trinity and the Trinity in unity, neither confusing the persons nor dividing the divine being.

For the Father is one person, the Son is another, and the Spirit is still another.

But the deity of the Father, Son, and Holy Spirit is one, equal in glory, coeternal in majesty.

What the Father is, the Son is, and so is the Holy Spirit.

Uncreated is the Father; uncreated is the Son; uncreated is the Spirit.

The Father is infinite; the Son is infinite; the Holy Spirit is infinite.

Eternal is the Father; eternal is the Son; eternal is the Spirit:

And yet there are not three eternal beings, but one who is eternal;

as there are not three uncreated and unlimited beings, but one who is uncreated and unlimited.

Almighty is the Father; almighty is the Son; almighty is the Spirit:

And yet there are not three almighty beings, but one who is almighty.

Thus the Father is God; the Son is God; the Holy Spirit is God:

And yet there are not three gods, but one God.

Thus the Father is Lord; the Son is Lord; the Holy Spirit is Lord:

And yet there are not three lords, but one Lord.

As Christian truth compels us to acknowledge each distinct person as God and Lord, so catholic religion forbids us to say that there are three gods or lords.

The Father was neither made nor created nor begotten;

the Son was neither made nor created, but was alone begotten of the Father;

the Spirit was neither made nor created, but is proceeding from the Father and the Son.

Thus there is one Father, not three fathers; one Son, not three sons; one Holy Spirit, not three spirits.

And in this Trinity, no one is before or after, greater or less than the other;

but all three persons are in themselves, coeternal and coequal; and so we must worship the Trinity in unity and the one God in three persons.

Whoever wants to be saved should think thus about the Trinity.

It is necessary for eternal salvation that one also faithfully believes that our Lord Jesus Christ became flesh.

For this is the true faith that we believe and confess: That our Lord Jesus Christ, God's Son, is both God and man.

He is God, begotten before all worlds from the being of the Father, and He is man, born in the world from the being of his mother -- existing fully as God, and fully as man with a rational soul and a human body; equal to the Father in divinity, subordinate to the Father in humanity.

Although He is God and man, He is not divided, but is one Christ.

He is united because God has taken humanity into himself; He does not transform deity into humanity. He is completely one in the unity of his person, without confusing his natures. For as the rational soul and body are one person, so the one Christ is God and man.

He suffered death for our salvation.
He descended into hell and rose again from the dead.
He ascended into heaven and is seated at the right hand of the Father.
He will come again to judge the living and the dead.
At his coming all people shall rise bodily to give an account of their own deeds.
Those who have done good will enter eternal life,
those who have done evil will enter eternal fire.
This is the catholic faith.

One cannot be saved without believing this firmly and faithfully.

Text prepared by the International Consultation on English Texts (ICET) and
the English Language Liturgical Consultation (ELLC). Reproduced by permission.

As seen in the examination of these creeds or statements of faith, there is a tendency to expand and change creeds to defend against and virtually close the doors to heresies that rear their heads throughout the existence of the creeds. Thus, just as doctrines spring into existence as an argument and defense against errors in the faith, so creeds change for the same purpose. This sprawl tends to be destructive for several reasons, not the least of which is expanding creeds take expanded time to understand and defend each area of belief. Man's ability to corrupt is endless and man's heresies are endless, thus, in time a creed could expand to become longer than the scripture itself. Expanding creeds take away from the other areas such as worship and prayer in our spiritual lives.

The simple answer to this is to understand if the Holy Spirit were guiding all of us we would be in one accord as a team under the same harness and reins. To worry about others and our defense against their errors is to weaken our own faith by spending less time with Him who guides us away from error. We cannot stop others from proceeding into error. We can only assure we will not go into error by fully understanding the few fast and hard beliefs held firm by those who came before; and using them as guidelines to ensure ourselves a clear view and understanding of the Christian faith.

When it comes to doctrine, to those that believe, no explanation is necessary, but for those who do not believe, no explanation will suffice.

A COMMON CREED EXPLAINED

I believe in God, the Father almighty, creator of heaven and earth.

GEN 1:1 In the beginning God created the heaven and the earth.
GEN 2:4 These are the generations of the heavens and of the earth when they were created, in the
day that the LORD God made the earth and the heavens,

I believe in Jesus Christ, his only Son, our Lord.

MAR 1:1 The beginning of the gospel of Jesus Christ, the Son of God;
LUK 2:11 For unto you is born this day in the city of David a Saviour, which is Christ the Lord.

He was conceived by the power of the Holy Spirit

MAT 1:18 Now the birth of Jesus Christ was on this wise: When as his mother Mary was espoused to
Joseph, before they came together, she was found with child of the Holy Ghost.

And born of the Virgin Mary.

MAT 1:18 Now the birth of Jesus Christ was on this wise: When as his mother Mary was espoused to
Joseph, before they came together, she was found with child of the Holy Ghost.
LUK 1:26 And in the sixth month the angel Gabriel was sent from God unto a city of Galilee, named
Nazareth, 27 To a virgin espoused to a man whose name was Joseph, of the house of David; and
the virgin's name was Mary. 28 And the angel came in unto her, and said, Hail, thou that art highly
favoured, the Lord is with thee: blessed art thou among women. 29 And when she saw him, she was
troubled at his saying, and cast in her mind what manner of salutation this should be. 30 And the

66

angel said unto her, Fear not, Mary: for thou hast found favour with God. 31 And, behold, thou shalt conceive in thy womb, and bring forth a son, and shalt call his name JESUS. 32 He shall be great, and shall be called the Son of the Highest: and the Lord God shall give unto him the throne of his father David:...

He suffered under Pontius Pilate

MAT 27:1 When the morning was come, all the chief priests and elders of the people took counsel against Jesus to put him to death: 2 And when they had bound him, they led him away, and delivered him to Pontius Pilate the governor.

Was crucified, died, and was buried.

MAT 27:35 And they crucified him, and parted his garments, casting lots: that it might be fulfilled which was spoken by the prophet, They parted my garments among them, and upon my vesture did they cast lots.

MAT 27:50 Jesus, when he had cried again with a loud voice, yielded up the ghost.

MAT 27:57 When the even was come, there came a rich man of Arimathaea, named Joseph, who also himself was Jesus' disciple: 58 He went to Pilate, and begged the body of Jesus. Then Pilate commanded the body to be delivered. 59 And when Joseph had taken the body, he wrapped it in a clean linen cloth, 60 And laid it in his own new tomb, which he had hewn out in the rock: and he rolled a great stone to the door of the sepulcher, and departed.

He descended into hell.*   *or "He descended to the dead."

1PE 3:18 For Christ also hath once suffered for sins, the just for the unjust, that he might bring us to God, being put to death in the flesh, but quickened by the Spirit: 19 By which also he went and

67

preached unto the spirits in prison;   *20 Which sometime were disobedient, when once the longsuffering of God waited in the days of Noah, while the ark was a preparing, wherein few, that is, eight souls were saved by water. 21 The like figure whereunto even baptism doth also now save us (not the putting away of the filth of the flesh, but the answer of a good conscience toward God,) by the resurrection of Jesus Christ:*

On the third day He rose again

LUK 24:6 He is not here, but is risen: remember how he spake unto you when he was yet in Galilee, 7 Saying, The Son of man must be delivered into the hands of sinful men, and be crucified, and the third day rise again. 8 And they remembered his words, 9 And returned from the sepulcher, and told all these things unto the eleven, and to all the rest.

He ascended into heaven

EPH 4:7 But unto every one of us is given grace according to the measure of the gift of Christ. 8 Wherefore he saith, When he ascended up on high, he led captivity captive, and gave gifts unto men. 9 Now that he ascended, what is it but that he also descended first into the lower parts of the earth? 10 He that descended is the same also that ascended up far above all heavens, that he might fill all things.

And is seated at the right hand of the Father

1 PE 3:22 Who is gone into heaven, and is on the right hand of God; angels and authorities and powers being made subject unto him.

He will come again to judge the living and the dead

68

ACT 17:30 And the times of this ignorance God winked at; but now commandeth all men every where to repent: 31   Because he hath appointed a day, in the which he will judge the world in righteousness by that man whom he hath ordained; whereof he hath given assurance unto all men, in that he hath raised him from the dead.

ROM 2:16 In the day when God shall judge the secrets of men by Jesus Christ according to my gospel.

ROM 14:10 But why dost thou judge thy brother? Or why dost thou set at naught thy brother? for we shall all stand before the judgment seat of Christ.   11 For it is written, As I live, saith the Lord, every knee shall bow to me, and every tongue shall confess to God. 12 So then every one of us shall give account of himself to God.

2TI 4:1 I charge thee therefore before God, and the Lord Jesus Christ, who shall judge the quick and the dead at his appearing and his kingdom; 2 Preach the word; be instant in season, out of season; reprove, rebuke, exhort with all longsuffering and doctrine.

I believe in the Holy Spirit

LUK 11:13 If ye then, being evil, know how to give good gifts unto your children: how much more shall your heavenly Father give the Holy Spirit to them that ask him?

The holy catholic (universal) Church

MAT 16:18 And I say also unto thee, That thou art Peter, and upon this rock I will build my church; and the gates of hell shall not prevail against it.

ACT 11:26 And when he had found him, he brought him unto Antioch. And it came to pass, that a whole year they assembled themselves with the church, and taught much people. And the disciples were called Christians first in Antioch.

1CO 1:2 Unto the church of God which is at Corinth, to them that are sanctified in Christ Jesus, called to be saints, with all that in every place call upon the name of Jesus Christ our Lord, both theirs and ours: 3 Grace be unto you, and peace, from God our Father, and from the Lord Jesus Christ.

The communion of saints

HEB 10:23 Let us hold fast the profession of our faith without wavering; for he is faithful that promised; 24 And let us consider one another to provoke unto love and to good works: 25 Not forsaking the assembling of ourselves together, as the manner of some is; but exhorting one another: and so much the more, as ye see the day approaching.

ACT 14:27 And when they were come, and had gathered the church together, they rehearsed all that God had done with them, and how he had opened the door of faith unto the Gentiles.

1CO 10:16 The cup of blessing which we bless, is it not the communion of the blood of Christ? The bread which we break, is it not the communion of the body of Christ? 17 For we being many are one bread, and one body: for we are all partakers of that one bread.

The forgiveness of sins

ACT 13:38 Be it known unto you therefore, men and brethren, that through this man is preached unto you the forgiveness of sins:

ACT 26:18 To open their eyes, and to turn them from darkness to light, and from the power of Satan unto God, that they may receive forgiveness of sins, and inheritance among them which are sanctified by faith that is in me.

70

EPH 1:7 In whom we have redemption through his blood, the forgiveness of sins, according to the riches of his grace;

The resurrection of the body

PHI 3:10 That I may know him, and the power of his resurrection, and the fellowship of his sufferings, being made conformable unto his death; 11 If by any means I might attain unto the resurrection of the dead.

1PE 1:3 Blessed be the God and Father of our Lord Jesus Christ, which according to his abundant mercy hath begotten us again unto a lively hope by the resurrection of Jesus Christ from the dead, 4 To an inheritance incorruptible, and undefiled, and that fadeth not away, reserved in heaven for you, 5 Who are kept by the power of God through faith unto salvation ready to be revealed in the last time.

And the life everlasting. Amen.

JOH 3:16 For God so loved the world, that he gave his only begotten Son, that whosoever believeth in him should not perish, but have everlasting life.

71

CHRIST and THE INCARNATION

It is at this point, most blessed, that we stumble. It is here at Christ's feet we fall and fail. It is with the words of adoration, love, and the description of Jesus that we perish in our intent. Even the Holy scriptures, though not in error, because of restrictions of word and language, fall so short as to utterly fail in any possible description of whom He is. Here, we destroy our own goals by attempting to somehow qualify or quantify His glory. With any words, no matter how well written, there will be an image formed, an idea set, a concept put in place, all of which will be incomplete and inadequate, and all of which must be transcended and un-known if His fullness is to be tasted.

Anything written will lead the reader into failure of knowing Him completely by placing in our feeble minds some restricted image even if it be holy and powerful. A description is no more the thing being described than a painting is the real sky or sea. One may point to something, describe it in detail, or paint a picture of it and still the image and words are completely useless when compared to the real and authentic item or the utility of the thing. It is more so with God, for He is infinite and cannot be captured in finite language, word, or color. Yet, for those who have not met Him, and for those who know Him only from others, I submit these lines as an enticement in hopes of encouraging you into a personal relationship of communion with Him. We must remember what He said of Himself. "TELL THEM, I AM."

When you hear that Jesus is begotten of God, beware lest the words make some inadequate thoughts of the flesh appears before your mind's eye.   The Tree of Life by St. Bonaventure

GEN 15:1 After these things the word of the LORD came unto Abram in a vision, saying, Fear not, Abram: I am thy shield, and thy exceeding great reward.

EXO 3:13 And Moses said unto God, Behold, when I come unto the children of Israel, and shall say unto them, The God of your fathers hath sent me unto you; and they shall say to me, What is his name? what shall I say unto them?

EXO 3:14 And God said unto Moses, I AM THAT I AM: and he said, Thus shalt thou say unto the children of Israel, I AM hath sent me unto you.

(In the person of Christ} a man has not become God; God has become man. (Cyril of Alexandria: Select Letters)

... for the Only Begotten Word of God has saved us by putting on our likeness. Suffering in the flesh, and rising from the dead, He revealed our nature as greater than death or corruption. What He achieved was beyond the ability of our condition, and what seemed to have been worked out in human weakness and by suffering was really stronger than men and a demonstration of the power that pertains to God. ...This was how He would be revealed as ennobling the nature of man in Himself by making {human nature} participate in his own sacred and divine honors. ... We must not think that He who descended into the limitation of manhood for our sake lost his inherent radiance and that transcendence that comes from his nature. No, He had this divine fullness even in the emptiness of our condition, and He enjoyed the highest eminence in humility, and held what belongs to him by nature (that is, to be worshipped by all) as a gift because of his humanity. Cyril of Alexandria

Now, everything is holy which is free of this world's defilement. And {such holiness} is in Christ by His very nature, just as it is in the Father; but in the holy disciples it is something adventitious, introduced from outside {through their participation in the Holy Spirit}, by means of the sanctification that comes by way of grace, and by means of splendid, virtuous living; for this is the manner in which one is fashioned to the divine, supramundane image. (The Image of God in Man according to Cyril of Alexandria)

Secrets of the incomprehensible wisdom of God, unknown to any beside Himselfl Man, sprung up only of a few days, wants to penetrate, and to set bounds to it. Who is it that hath known the mind of the Lord, or who hath been His counselor? Quotations from Jeanne-Marie Bouvier de la Motte-Guyon

The Incarnation is not a union of wills dependent upon some fragile and inconsistent human response toward Christ. Grace cannot depend upon anything, certainly not the deficiencies of the best of human will. Grace must be unconditional, depending on nothing from, in, or of us. The Incarnation must therefore be an amalgam of Christ with man. This union, although never forced upon us, must be stronger than we and stronger further than any human act or choice. The incarnate Word coming into human conditions and limitations was enacted in order to radically change, alter, and restore them, without destroying them.

God remains God and his man is still man, but after Christ has come upon us we are charged with divine power. Only then are we, the believer, capable of restoring or being restored to the fullness of life as we share in it sacramentally with Him. It then becomes the ultimate paradox that in the strictest Trinitarian view, God offers praise and prayer to himself through us. But, then, who else would be worthy to praise Him and commune with Him except it be He? God in us as Christ has imbued us with Himself through perfect grace has now made it possible for us to approach the Father in love and adoration.

... He transmits the grace of sonship even to us..., insofar as human nature had first achieved this possibility in Him. (On the Unity of Christ)

IN REMEMBRANCE OF HIM

It is in the remembrance, celebration, and meditation on Christ's incarnation and act of sacrifice for mankind that many fall short. On the Body and Blood we should meditate and understand the meaning and depth of the love God has for us. The meaning of the bread and wine escapes us because the full gravity of the sacrifice escapes our secular and mundane hearts. Take, for example, a worldly token such as a dollar bill. Look at the piece of paper you hold and ask yourself what it is worth. The answer is one dollar. Yet the paper and ink are worth nothing. The dollar is the value it represents. The dollar is a symbol of that amount of worth ascribed by our government to a worthless piece of paper. Thus it is with the bread and wine of our communion. Jesus himself gave us the worth of the symbols of the bread and wine when he said:

MAT 26:26 And as they were eating, Jesus took bread, and blessed it, and brake it, and gave it to the disciples, and said, Take, eat; this is my body. 27 And he took the cup, and gave thanks, and gave it to them, saying, Drink ye all of it; 28 For this is my blood of the new testament, which is shed for many for the remission of sins. 29 But I say unto you, I will not drink henceforth of this fruit of the vine, until that day when I drink it new with you in my Father's kingdom.

It is no longer I who live but Christ who lives in me. We say this, and we read this, but we do not act as if we believe it. We do not understand until His grace floods us and possesses us. It is because we have never sought to be filled to such a degree that only He exists in us. It is not the bread that is the Eucharist. It is Christ in us that is the Eucharist, for He is our Thanksgiving, and we are His, and He is the Thanksgiving of God. We should not worry about taking the Eucharist. No one is worthy to partake. But the scriptures tell us to partake worthily, the writings do not say to partake if you are worthy. Who is worthy to partake of Christ except Christ alone? We are told that we partake worthily if we discern the body and blood of Christ. Do we know who He is, and why His body and blood were given up? Then we have partaken worthily, because if we know Him, and if He is in us, then it is He who is partaking as only He can partake of something so holy as the body and blood of God Himself.

What is the value of this bread and wine? Whether one believes in transubstantiation, wherein the bread and wine literally become the physical and corporeal body and blood of Christ, or if one believes the bread and wine are symbols of the body and blood of our Lord, the value ascribed to them is what they represent and what they are worth, thus and should be treated the same. If one wishes to argue this point let us take his money and burn it since it is simply a pile of worthless paper, already printed upon. What is the worth of the Body of God? What is the worth of His blood? What is the worth of the sacrifice of a perfect man? What is the worth of the life of God? The symbols are worth the same as the things they represent because Christ himself gave them their worth. Do not be afraid for He is worthy of all praise, glory, and honor, and He is in us. This is the Eucharist of God. As Jesus is Eucharist to us, we should be Eucharist to one another. This goes back to the two commandments — love God and love our neighbor as ourselves.

1CO 11:25 After the same manner also he took the cup, when he had supped, saying, This cup is the new testament in my blood: this do ye, as oft as ye drink it, in remembrance of me. 26 For as often as ye eat this bread, and drink this cup, ye do shew the Lord's death till he come. 27 Wherefore whosoever shall eat this bread, and drink this cup of the Lord, unworthily, shall be guilty of the body and blood of the Lord. 28 But let a man examine himself, and so let him eat of that bread, and drink of that cup. 29 For he that eateth and drinketh unworthily, eateth and drinketh damnation to himself, not discerning the Lord's body.

If we could do one small piece to make ourselves worthy, we could not "count it all Grace".

The goodness of man is like children jumping to see who can come closest to the moon. What difference can an inch make in such a shortfall?   Russ Martin

WHO IS HE?

Who is this God we seek? What is his character? If He created all things and by Him and through Him all things exist, what can we say about Him? What does He tell us about himself? Here are the names by which He is called in the scriptures. Each name reflects part of His character. By these names we know Him.

THE FIRST AND LAST: Isa. 44:6, 48:12.

ADONAI: Lord or Master

ABHIR: Mighty One

ANCIENT OF DAYS: Dan. 7:9, 13, 22.

CHRIST: Messiah, The Anointed One

DESPOTES: Lord

EL ELYON: Most High

EYALUTH: Strength

ELOHIM: God (a plural noun)

EL ROI: God of Seeing

EL SHADDAI: God Almighty, God All Sufficient.

EL-OLAM: Everlasting God

EL-BERITH: God of the Covenant

EL-GIBHOR: Mighty God

GAOL: Redeemer

HUPSISTOS: Highest

JEHOVAH: LORD **Yahweh** is the covenant name of God "The Self-Existent One," "I AM WHO I AM" or 'I WILL BE WHO I WILL BE" **I AM:** "Before Abraham was, I AM," John 8:58.

JEHOVAH-JIREH: The Lord will Provide.

JEHOVAH-ROPHE: "The Lord Who Heals

JEHOVAH-NISSI: The Lord Our Banner

JEHOVAH-M'KADDESH: The Lord Who Sanctifies

JEHOVAH-SHALOM: The Lord Our Peace

JEHOVAH ELOHIM: LORD God

JEHOVAH-TSIDKENU: The Lord Our Righteousness

JEHOVAH-ROHI: The Lord Our Shepherd

JEHOVAH-SHAMMAH: The Lord is There (Ezek. 48:35).

JEHOVAH-SABAOTH: The Lord of Hosts

JESUS: Derived from the Hebrew "Joshua" (Y'shua) JEHOVAH IS SALVATION

KADOSH: Holy One

KURIOS: Lord

LOGOS: The Word of God

MAGEN: Shield

MY SHEPHERD Psa. 23, 79:13,

SHAPHAT: Judge

SOTER: Savior

TSADDIQ: Righteous One

THEOS: God

THEOTES: Godhead

Wonderful, Counselor, Mighty God, Everlasting Father, Prince of Peace (Isa. 9:6).

YESHA: (Y'shua) Savior

ZUR: God our Rock

I am Alpha and Omega, the beginning and the ending, saith the Lord, which is, and which was, and which is to come, the Almighty. REV 1:8

PRESENTING CHRIST IN US TO THE WORLD

Christ has no body now on earth but yours, no hands but yours, no feet but yours, yours are the eyes through which is to look out Christ's compassion to the world: yours are the feet with which he is to go out about doing good; yours are the hands with which he is to bless men now. St. Teresa of Avila

Christ's living in me is at the same time himself and myself. From this moment until I am united with Him in one spirit there is no longer any contradiction implied by the fact that we are different persons. He remains, naturally and physically, the son of God ... I remain the singular person that I am. But mystically and spiritually Christ lives in me from the moment that I am united to Him in his death and resurrection... Thomas Merton

The story of Mary holds within it, several deep lessons for the Christian mystic. Even before the great schism between the Orthodox and Roman churches, Mary held a place in the minds and hearts of the Christian church. Later, in church history, in a move to balance what was felt to be an over-emphasis on Mary and her status, the Protestant church began to diminish her status until she is now considered little more than a willing incubator for Jesus. Polarization is an all too human reaction, which leads us, in many cases, to fully reject a doctrine and even a person when we believe it, or they, are in error. The error may hold only a part of what is presented, but the rejection is full. Thus large areas of truth are thrown out with areas of error.

The Bible tells us she will be called blessed, but many do not call her anything at all. The majority of Protestant believers ignore Mary. It is the overcompensation to avoid the recurrence of the error. Throwing truth out with error, the baby that got tossed out in the bathwater of error this time happened to be the Mother of Jesus. I do not support an extreme elevation or veneration of Mary or

80

of any creature for that matter, since such a view would cloud the vision of the preeminence of Christ. But, neither do I agree with the place to which most Protestant churches have resigned her.

Although it is true grace shed on someone does not indicate moral or spiritual status, it is also true God had a plan for salvation from the foundations of the world and in His plan, Mary had a place. As people of faith, Mary's story has a deep and significant meaning for us. Grace is given without, and many times, in spite of spiritual condition. It was not Mary's state or condition but the willingness of her decision that drew the sovereign will of God. In this vein the early fathers found something so fascinating and deeply spiritual about the story of Mary they elevated her to a venerated status. As we look closer into the story of Mary we will see she is the template and prototype of the true mystical experience. Her experience is the key and summation of the entire Christian process. In her we find our spiritual likeness, our history, and our story. In the story of Mary the mystical life is foretold.

LUKE 1:35 And the angel answered and said unto her, The Holy Ghost shall come upon thee, and the power of the Highest shall overshadow thee: therefore also that holy thing which shall be born of thee shall be called the Son of God. 37 For with God nothing shall be impossible. 38 And Mary said, Behold the handmaid of the Lord; be it unto me according to thy word. And the angel departed from her. 41 And it came to pass, that, when Elisabeth heard the salutation of Mary, the babe leaped in her womb; and Elisabeth was filled with the Holy Ghost: 42 And she spake out with a loud voice, and said, Blessed art thou among women, and blessed is the fruit of thy womb. 43 And whence is this to me, that the mother of my Lord should come to me? 44 For, lo, as soon as the voice of thy salutation sounded in mine ears, the babe leaped in my womb for joy. 45 And blessed is she that believed: for there shall be a performance of those things, which were told her from the Lord. 46 And Mary said, My soul doth magnify the Lord, 47 And my spirit hath rejoiced in God my Saviour.

81

LUK 1:48 For he hath regarded the low estate of his handmaiden: for, behold, from henceforth all generations shall call me blessed. 49 For he that is mighty hath done to me great things; and holy is his name. 50 And his mercy is on them that fear him from generation to generation. 51 He hath shewed strength with his arm; he hath scattered the proud in the imagination of their hearts.   52 He hath put down the mighty from their seats, and exalted them of low degree.

In His grace, God chose Mary, a young woman with no obvious attributes that set her apart from hundreds of others. In her own words, she was someone who counted herself as a lowly maiden. In his power and mercy He came to her. His spirit was on her and in her and He communed with her within her heart and soul.   God, being out of time and space, had a plan for creation before He created. This also includes the incarnation. Creation was created for Jesus and through Jesus. The plan for creation was completed in the mind of God before the act of creating. Therefore, Mary was in God's plan for the birth of Jesus before creation, but because of free will she had acquiescence. It was because of her free will and the obedience that followed from it she was blessed. We cannot know why Mary was chosen and set apart. God has always used men and women who seemed common and ordinary to do great things. So it was with the mother of God. Mary, by believing the child in her was indeed sent and fathered by the Holy Spirit of God and set in her virgin body for the redemption of man, became the first Christian.

" The Holy Ghost shall come upon thee, and the power of the Highest shall overshadow thee: therefore also that holy thing which shall be born of thee shall be called the Son of God." Luke 1:35

It was not through doctrine or church that they met but through a real and powerful personal communion. This is the essence of the mystical experience. God draws us and woos us to Him and in our desire to be with Him we are allowed an intimate communion with Him. In this spiritual state of togetherness with God, the Holy Spirit of God implants Christ in our spiritual wombs. Christ forms in us, grows in us, moves in us and through us until we give birth to Him through our hearts and souls and show Him to the world in our love and actions with spontaneous acts of love and serving. It is through a heart and mind that calls out to Him and declares, "Behold the handmaid of the Lord; be it unto me according to thy word." Only in this can we contain God's Spirit. Only in this will God hold us. By this alone comes the world's greatest experience. What we do not realize in our simplicity is each time Christ is birthed in us we are experiencing the mystical equivalent of the incarnation once again. Each time we nurture Him in us and show Him forth to others, we have become Mary and the great incarnation has come upon us.

ISA 9:6 For unto us a child is born, unto us a son is given: and the government shall be upon his shoulder: and his name shall be called Wonderful, Counsellor, The mighty God, The everlasting Father, The Prince of Peace. 7 Of the increase of his government and peace there shall be no end, upon the throne of David, and upon his kingdom, to order it, and to establish it with judgment and with justice from henceforth even for ever. The zeal of the LORD of hosts will perform this.

It is for this event that even if man had not fallen, still Christ would have come. He is the crown of mankind. He is the crowning of creation. He was destined from the foundation of creation to be the one and only avenue for the union of God and man. Such a union going far beyond any understanding communion could bring. Thus, we may commune with God but Christ lives in us, in a state that is distinct yet in union.

GOD WORSHIP AND OBEDIENCE

As the world becomes more sophisticated man tends to rely on his own understanding, as limited as it may be. In this environment, threads and smatterings of Christianity, Eastern religions, new age, and ancient beliefs mix into a stew of nonsense. One of the main beliefs to rear its old head is pantheism, the belief God is in all things and is all things. Out of this religious structure one concludes God is an all-invasive and ever-present energy. It is surprising how many Christians lean toward this conclusion. But, this outlook does not support the need for worship or obedience.

83

If God is everything one can easily make the leap of logic that God is energy. He or his creations would exist as patterns of energy. Energy has no mind, no likes, no dislikes, no goals, no ability to decide, no conscience, and no love. In this world, God would not care. There would be no need to worship God since He would have no mind to care or appreciate our actions. There would be no need for obedience to the will of God since He would have no will. We would only have to worry about understanding the pattern and flow of the energy in order to use it correctly. For maximum results, we would not want to go against the energy, whatever we would define it to be. There would be no sin because there would be no rule or opinion from God to miss or dismiss.

Pantheism makes no distinctions between the creature and the creator. They are the same. Thus God is lowered to the level of the lowest of creatures and the creature raised to the status of God. For how can God be divisible? Like water, any part of God would have the same nature as the whole. Any portion of an infinite has infinity within it. How then can we say this twig or that worm, which are without thought and love, can be God? If, however, God had just one thought, one wish, one desire, or one preference, the framework of pantheism would come tumbling down, and with it, disobedience and sin would come into being.

PARADOX OF THE WAY

Individual Will, Predestination, and God's Path for our Lives

MAT 5:44 But I say unto you, Love your enemies, bless them that curse you, do good to them that hate you, and pray for them which despitefully use you, and persecute you; 45 That ye may be the children of your Father, which is in heaven: for he maketh his sun to rise on the evil and on the good, and sendeth rain on the just and on the unjust.

EPH 1:3 Blessed be the God and Father of our Lord Jesus Christ, who hath blessed us with all spiritual blessings in heavenly places in Christ: 4 According as he hath chosen us in him before the foundation of the world, that we should be holy and without blame before him in love: 5 Having predestinated us unto the adoption of children by Jesus Christ to himself, according to the good pleasure of his will, 6 To the praise of the glory of his grace, wherein he hath made us accepted in the beloved. EPH 1:8 Wherein he hath abounded toward us in all wisdom and prudence; 9 Having made known unto us the mystery of his will, according to his good pleasure which he hath purposed in himself: 10 That in the dispensation of the fullness of times he might gather together in one all things in Christ, both which are in heaven, and which are on earth; even in him: 11 In whom also we have obtained an inheritance, being predestinated according to the purpose of him who worketh all things after the counsel of his own will: 12 That we should be to the praise of his glory, who first trusted in Christ.

With limited insight and finite minds, we enter into arguments about God and his infinite plan. We debate and denominations split over our feeble ideas of free will, foreknowledge, predestination, and self-determination. Never could we hope to understand the depth and complexity of God, but argue it passionately, we will.

Does God have a plan for us? Did He make us for a reason? Are we here to fulfill His plan of salvation and light in the world? I am not asking if God "needs" us to fulfill His plan. I am asking if we have a place in His plan? Do we have an individual purpose? Is obedience a choice? Does one have free will? Is free will necessary in order to love? It seems that both views, predestination and foreknowledge, must be correct. As mutually exclusive as predestination and foreknowledge may appear upon first sight, they must somehow co-exist in the plan of God. Like a river flowing through a valley, we live on the path we are placed upon from birth. Along this path of life we encounter people and circumstances related to the timing of our birth and path. We have no acquiescence in this. Our starting point in time, place of birth, social placement, financial status, abilities, intelligence range, and other items are things we cannot control. They are functions of timing, circumstances, or genetics.

We are born into a family at a time and in a place with certain strengths and weaknesses none of which we can control. We are set on a general path of life based on these attributes and resources. Some of these determine what life has in store for us. Like the landscape, terrain, rocks, boulders, eddies, and currents of the river, we will endure what happens to us along the way. The way we flow with or in spite of the obstacles is up to us. Although we are made in a certain way, we know we may choose to give in to sin or resist the Devil. There are six billion people on this planet. Each one of them has free will, although one may argue to what degree. Six billion people make choices throughout the day that affect others. From our vantage point it may look as if we spin our wheel of fortune and take what life has to offer. Indeed, that is how life affects us at times, but our view is a microcosmic myopia. From a heavenly arena it may be in perfect order. Some would say with faith, grace, and salvation issuing from the throne of God, all things are in His hands. It is true nothing in the plan of salvation is left undone.

David, looking ahead into the brilliant light of God's plan wrote: *PSA 116:12 What shall I render unto the LORD for all his benefits toward me? 13 I will take the cup of salvation, and call upon the name of the LORD.*

Thus we take and drink the cup of His salvation and we call upon the name of the Lord.

ROM 10:13 For whosoever shall call upon the name of the Lord shall be saved.

One could easily cross into a fatalistic predestinationalism if it weren't for the fact that our response to the plight of the world is in our hands. We exercise our choice to forgive, hate, love, help, or hinder each moment of every day. It is our free will. A plan must be put to use - and that is our place

86

in God's plan, to take what is offered and decide to forgive, have gratitude, and love. This can be a most difficult thing when facing the death or injury of a loved one, or betrayal from a friend. I cannot say with certainty that any of those things are in God's plan. I can say they came from the interactions of the free will of men. The one thing I am certain of is that God is leading us in the direction of salvation and relationship with Him. If God's plan for us is general and expansive, such as to love others and to love Him, then in those times of trials we should run to Him for solace and strength. If His plan is specific, such as a particular profession, marriage to a particular person, and such, we should run to Him for advice. In either case, our place is with God.

This is how the plan of salvation and man's place therein seem to fit together in a tapestry of predestination and foreknowledge, but in the end we must admit our inability to know the mind of God. Did God make us to succeed or fail? Did He create some to endure hell forever while giving some eternal life from the start? As the scriptures read, (reading more accurately in the ancient Greek), He has predestined salvation for us in Christ. It does not say He predestined us for salvation. How much control we have and how much is all in the hands of God, we will not know until we can view our life in one long scene from the portals of heaven and ask God face to face. I have a feeling at that point it will not really matter. These issues have forced us off task too often. They have clogged our minds with "unknowables" and, through our pride, we have been led to take sides and travel side roads, and defend our vague ideas to the point we have lost sight of Him whose plan we argue.

1CO 8:1 … Knowledge puffeth up, but charity edifieth. 2 And if any man think that he knoweth any thing, he knoweth nothing yet as he ought to know. 3 But if any man love God, the same is known of him.

LUK 11:42 But woe unto you, Pharisees! for ye tithe mint and rue and all manner of herbs, and pass over judgment and the love of God: these ought ye to have done, and not to leave the other undone.

43 Woe unto you, Pharisees! for ye love the uppermost seats in the synagogues, and greetings in the markets. 44 Woe unto you, scribes and Pharisees, hypocrites! for ye are as graves which appear not, and the men that walk over them are not aware of them. 45 Then answered one of the lawyers, and said unto him, Master, thus saying thou reproachest us also. 46 And he said, Woe unto you also, ye lawyers! for ye lade men with burdens grievous to be borne, and ye yourselves touch not the burdens with one of your fingers.

HEB 5:11 Of whom we have many things to say, and hard to be uttered, seeing ye are dull of hearing .12 For when for the time ye ought to be teachers, ye have need that one teach you again which be the first principles of the oracles of God; and are become such as have need of milk, and not of strong meat. 13 For every one that useth milk is unskillful in the word of righteousness: for he is a babe. 14 But strong meat belongeth to them that are of full age, even those who by reason of use have their senses exercised to discern both good and evil. 6:1 Therefore leaving the principles of the doctrine of Christ, let us go on unto perfection; not laying again the foundation of repentance from dead works, and of faith toward God, 2 Of the doctrine of baptisms, and of laying on of hands, and of resurrection of the dead, and of eternal judgment. 3 And this will we do, if God permit.

ROM 3:19 Now we know that what things soever the law saith, it saith to them who are under the law: that every mouth may be stopped, and all the world may become guilty before God. 20 Therefore by the deeds of the law there shall no flesh be justified in his sight: for by the law is the knowledge of sin. 21 But now the righteousness of God without the law is manifested, being witnessed by the law and the prophets; 22 Even the righteousness of God which is by faith of Jesus Christ unto all and upon all them that believe: for there is no difference:23 For all have sinned, and come short of the glory of God; 24 Being justified freely by his grace through the redemption that is in Christ Jesus

We have set in place doctrines with names to keep out those who disagree with things we cannot prove. We create denominations each time we accent a piece of the truth to the exclusion of the whole. We part ways through politics and power as disagreements arise as to who should control the church or how control is maintained. Where is God in all of this? He is not in the work we do to convert others to our denomination or convince others of our way. He is in His word, working to save the lost soul, and He is in the hearts of those who believe in Him. Denominationalism is not Christianity. It is a study of the beliefs of a group usually based on the views of a single man.

Furthermore, denominations are based partly on personality and preferences. In a general way, there are certain personalities drawn toward certain denominations. Many times we are raised in a denomination or church and there we stay out of a sense of family or loyalty, but if people were to be set free from those things we would find like attracts like. It is simply a function of personality that a kinetic, effusive person is not going to be comfortable in a quiet, liturgically driven church. Likewise, an orderly, structured, quiet person will find a noisy, free flowing, spontaneous service disturbing. Some churches have overcome this problem by having two or more services of differing types. The beliefs are that same, they are simply expressed differently. In this natural grouping it can be seen denominations can be a matter of how to express one's beliefs as much as what the beliefs are.

Some churches break down membership across socio-economic levels where the wealthy tend to gather in one church and the poor attend another church. It is a generally accepted rule of society that most individuals tend to stay within one or two social classes of their upbringing. This assumes a five to seven class system of income and lifestyle. The five class system breakdown is comprised of lower, lower-middle, middle, upper-middle, and upper classes. Since it tends to stress most people to ascend or descend more than two social levels, it stands to reason intermingling for any length of time would be uncomfortable to some. We tend to stay with our own kind, and that tends to include class groups also. This is the worldly man, who judges according to riches, and not the spiritual man, who sees the love of God in others equally. None of this is to say there are not more errors and heresies in certain sects and denominations. Some have more solid theologies than others, however, keeping with the basics of the creed presented will help avoid pitfalls of theology and bring most other issues to a point of view or political structure.

JAM 2:2 For if there come unto your assembly a man with a gold ring, in goodly apparel, and here come in also a poor man in vile raiment; 3 And ye have respect to him that weareth the gay clothing, and say unto him, Sit thou here in a good place; and say to the poor, Stand thou there, or sit here under my footstool: 4 Are ye not then partial in yourselves, and are become judges of evil thoughts? 5 Hearken, my beloved brethren, Hath not God chosen the poor of this world rich in faith, and heirs of the kingdom which he hath promised to them that love him? 6 But ye have despised the poor. Do not rich men oppress you, and draw you before the judgment seats? 7 Do not they blaspheme that worthy name by the which ye are called? 8 If ye fulfil the royal law according to the scripture, Thou shalt love thy neighbour as thyself, ye do well:

Denominations and church attendance can fall into man-made categories. Categories and denominations sprang from man, not God. Our purpose is not to belong to a denomination. It is to belong to God. Again, man falls into a Pharisee mindset, ignoring the reason of our salvation and arguing the minutiae.

This is not to say we should avoid church. We need the reinforcement and support of fellow Christians. In our churches, let us stand out as those who love and support others in their search for God.

HEB 10:23 Let us hold fast the profession of our faith without wavering; (for he is faithful that promised;) 24 And let us consider one another to provoke unto love and to good works: 25 Not forsaking the assembling of ourselves together, as the manner of some is; but exhorting one another: and so much the more, as ye see the day approaching.

90

It is in this vein I find myself stopped short and lacking. Having letters of someone learned and having seen the zeal to study doctrine day and night, I became as one having a tourniquet around his neck, with head and heart separate, I had no ability to transmute knowledge into wisdom.

2TI 3:7 Ever learning, and never able to come to the knowledge of the truth.

It is because knowledge of anything other than Christ can become superfluous. We must strive to keep the three legs of our Christian journey in balance. The three legs of Christian life are Worship, Study, and Prayer. Our worship must be pure and upward reaching, not simply entertainment, good music, or fiery preaching but full of the passion of His passion, His life, His purpose, His nature, and His words. Our study should be more about Him and His character and less about social ideas. Our prayers should be a never-ceasing desire to commune with God and to know Him and His will. With God's character in us, we will know what He would have us do.

We should avoid useless and divisive doctrine, which is impossible to prove as well as those having little or nothing to do with our relationship to God and salvation. We should ask ourselves as an example, "If the doctrine of predestination or foreknowledge was true, would I still serve Him?" If the answer is yes, it is not worth spending much time to study it. The time used to read about others opinions on that subject should be used to seek God.

We must strive to keep our prayer life in balance between Discursive prayer and Contemplative prayer. In discursive prayer we carry on a dialogue between the Lord and ourselves. The problem in this type of prayer is we tend to do all of the talking. We bring a wish list before the throne. We repeat our requests as if He did not hear us the first time. We beg God to fill our requests, as if we could possibly know what is best in the light of eternity. We seldom listen to His answer. In

91

contemplative prayer we stay silent and listen to the Lord. We think about Him and His glory. We learn to be still inside so we may hear His soft, beckoning voice.

Prayer is not for us to change the mind of God, but for us to be conformed to His will.

PART THREE

TO REACH THE MOUNTAIN YOU MUST FIRST CLEAR THE PATH

Up to this point, we have spent time clarifying who God is and what we believe. Even Satan and his demons know who Christ is but this knowledge has not freed them. The knowledge never made it from head to heart. Their knowledge never became truth. Will we take the knowledge and make it truth in our lives? Will we become more righteous than Satan?

MAT 7:21 Not every one that saith unto me, Lord, Lord, shall enter into the kingdom of heaven; but he that doeth the will of my Father which is in heaven. 22 Many will say to me in that day, Lord, Lord, have we not prophesied in thy name? and in thy name have cast out devils? and in thy name done many wonderful works? 23 And then will I profess unto them, I never knew you: depart from me, ye that work iniquity.

MAR 5:2 And when he was come out of the ship, immediately there met him out of the tombs a man with an unclean spirit, 3 Who had his dwelling among the tombs; and no man could bind him, no, not with chains: 4 Because that he had been often bound with fetters and chains, and the chains had been plucked asunder by him, and the fetters broken in pieces: neither could any man tame him. 5 And always, night and day, he was in the mountains, and in the tombs, crying, and cutting himself with stones. 6 But when he saw Jesus afar off, he ran and worshipped him, 7 And cried with a loud voice, and said, What have I to do with thee, Jesus, thou Son of the most high God? I adjure thee by God, that thou torment me not.

Knowledge alone does nothing to change the heart of man or demon. Only being with God and communing with Him will alter our natures and only then according to our ability to yield to His spirit through obedience. Acting on knowledge as truth is faith, and faith is the key to heaven. Satan knows the truth of who God is but He does not act on it. Satan knows God but has no faith.

In espousing the following point I know I will incur the wrath of many. However, if we think about it carefully we will find it to be true. Church attendance, obedience to the law, knowledge of the Scriptures, prayer if empty repetition, even worship if it is empty of spirit, will not change the heart of man. Only by being in God's presence can we hope to get to know Him intimately and be changed by exposure to Him; as a child is changed and molded by the parent. Our churches have lost the way back to God. The people are not being told what it takes to live a full spiritual life. Because of this our churches are dying and people are suffering. We go to church, assemble together, read scripture, sing songs, pray, and leave. Seldom, if ever, do we simply sit and wait on the Spirit to come, to speak, to work in us.

We have been glimpsing God through Holy Scripture and doctrine. This is like trying to know someone by looking at his portrait or reading his letters. It is a facsimile and not the real person. We can get to know certain things about them and only those on a superficial level. We can come to admire them and even understand certain traits of their nature, but it is not the same as having a conversation and spending time with them. Most people, even ministers and priests, have reduced a relationship with God to a study session. Their time in prayer is when they tell God their troubles, needs, and greed. It takes time to listen and we don't seem to have time for God these days. This is not the way our relationship with God was intended to be. However, now that we have an understanding as to who He is and what He is like, we can make a decision if we wish to know Him better. We can, if we choose, extend our relationship to a state of intimacy. Knowing by experience is quite different than knowing by reading. The things we have learned about God and His nature will help lead us toward Him and keep us on the right path.

94

Scripture and the doctrine that springs from it are to inform man of the plan, purpose, and person of God and to direct, guide, and inspire man.

But, if scripture and doctrine were enough we could have kept the law and could have been justified by the law. Having no sin found in man under the law, there would have been no need for Christ to have come and die. But, scripture and doctrine are not enough and the heart of man has not changed. Even Adam, who spent time with God and had a relationship with Him fell, sinned, and died. What chance do we have? We have someone who paid the price of death for us and we have the spirit of God moving inside us, working to guide us and make us into His image. We have hope because we have forgiveness.

HEB 2:17 Wherefore in all things it behooved him to be made like unto his brethren, that he might be a merciful and faithful high priest in things pertaining to God, to make reconciliation for the sins of the people. 18 For in that he himself hath suffered being tempted, he is able to succour them that are tempted.

We no longer have to rely on ourselves to keep the law. We rely on the one who gave the law to keep us. Now we study the word to know about Him and His ways because we love the one who saved us. Scripture now takes on a new dimension.

2TI 3:16 All scripture is given by inspiration of God, and is profitable for doctrine, for reproof, for correction, for instruction in righteousness: 17 That the man of God may be perfect, thoroughly furnished unto all good works.

2TI 4:1 I charge thee therefore before God, and the Lord Jesus Christ, who shall judge the quick and the dead at his appearing and his kingdom; 2 Preach the word; be instant in season, out of season;

95

reprove, rebuke, exhort with all longsuffering and doctrine. 3 For the time will come when they will not endure sound doctrine; but after their own lusts shall they heap to themselves teachers, having itching ears; 4 And they shall turn away their ears from the truth, and shall be turned unto fables.

DEU 32:1 Give ear, O ye heavens, and I will speak; and hear, O earth, the words of my mouth. 2 My doctrine shall drop as the rain, my speech shall distil as the dew, as the small rain upon the tender herb, and as the showers upon the grass: 3 Because I will publish the name of the LORD: ascribe ye greatness unto our God. 4 He is the Rock, his work is perfect: for all his ways are judgment: a God of truth and without iniquity, just and right is he.

PRO 4:1 Hear, ye children, the instruction of a father, and attend to know understanding. 2 For I give you good doctrine, forsake ye not my law. 3 For I was my father's son, tender and only beloved in the sight of my mother. 4 He taught me also, and said unto me, Let thine heart retain my words: keep my commandments, and live. 5 Get wisdom, get understanding: forget it not; neither decline from the words of my mouth. 6 Forsake her not, and she shall preserve thee: love her, and she shall keep thee.

MAR 4:1 And he began again to teach by the seaside: and there was gathered unto him a great multitude, so that he entered into a ship, and sat in the sea; and the whole multitude was by the sea on the land. 2 And he taught them many things by parables, and said unto them in his doctrine,

MAR 12:38 And he said unto them in his doctrine, Beware of the scribes, which love to go in long clothing, and love salutations in the marketplaces, 39 And the chief seats in the synagogues, and the uppermost rooms at feasts: 40 Which devour widows' houses, and for a pretence make long prayers: these shall receive greater damnation.

JOH 7:16 Jesus answered them, and said, My doctrine is not mine, but his that sent me. 17 If any man will do his will, he shall know of the doctrine, whether it be of God, or whether I speak of myself. 18 He that speaketh of himself seeketh his own glory: but he that seeketh his glory that sent him, the same is true, and no unrighteousness is in him.

ACT 2:41 Then they that gladly received his word were baptized: and the same day there were added unto them about three thousand souls. 42 And they continued steadfastly in the apostles' doctrine and fellowship, and in breaking of bread, and in prayers.

ROM 6:16 Know ye not, that to whom ye yield yourselves servants to obey, his servants ye are to whom ye obey; whether of sin unto death, or of obedience unto righteousness? 17 But God be thanked, that ye were the servants of sin, but ye have obeyed from the heart that form of doctrine which was delivered you. Being then made free from sin, ye became the servants of righteousness.

1TI 4:6 If thou put the brethren in remembrance of these things, thou shalt be a good minister of Jesus Christ, nourished up in the words of faith and of good doctrine, whereunto thou hast attained.

TRAPS AND SNARES ALONG THE PATH

Hate, resentment, and anger

As we approach Him we will find our hearts will open to Him and we will begin to recognize His presence in our hearts and lives more easily. We will get to know God on an intimate level. Unfortunately, there are things that will stop us in our tracks. Hate, resentment, and anger can destroy our journey. They are contrary to the heart and wishes of God. These emotions stick like glue to the heart of man. They hang on us like weights around our necks, impeding us on the journey. They will wear us down, fatigue our steps, and halt our progress. Sadly, these things, hate, resentment and anger are some of the last obstacles to be overcome.

Anger: excessive emotion or passion aroused by a sense of injury or wrong; wrath; to provoke to resentment; excite to wrath; enrage.   Webster's New School and Office Dictionary

Hate: to dislike intensely: abhor: detest: intense aversion.   Webster's New School and Office Dictionary

Resentment: strong anger or displeasure: deep sense of injury.   Webster's New School and Office Dictionary

Hate, anger, and resentment are interwoven emotions. They eat at us and consume us slowly, like an acid; they rot us from the inside. They draw our minds to the pain from injuries done in the past. The pain holds us hostage in the past, by the pain we feel in the present. We hearken to the past and our minds dwell there. Letting go of the pain is not so easy, and although I do not want this to evolve into a book on psychology, we must realize healing and forgiveness are needed.

PHI 2:3 Let nothing be done through strife or vainglory; but in lowliness of mind let each esteem other better than themselves. 4 Look not every man on his own things, but every man also on the things of others. 5 Let this mind be in you, which was also in Christ Jesus:

JAM 3:16 For where envying and strife is, there is confusion and every evil work.

LEV 19:17 Thou shalt not hate thy brother in thine heart: thou shalt in any wise rebuke thy neighbour, and not suffer sin upon him. 18 Thou shalt not avenge, nor bear any grudge against the children of thy people, but thou shalt love thy neighbour as thyself: I am the LORD.

PSA 34:21 Evil shall slay the wicked: and they that hate the righteous shall be desolate. 22 The LORD redeemeth the soul of his servants: and none of them that trust in him shall be desolate.

MAT 5:43 Ye have heard that it hath been said, Thou shalt love thy neighbour, and hate thine enemy. 44 But I say unto you, Love your enemies, bless them that curse you, do good to them that hate you, and pray for them which despitefully use you, and persecute you; 45 That ye may be the children of your Father which is in heaven: for he maketh his sun to rise on the evil and on the good, and sendeth rain on the just and on the unjust.

LUK 6:22 Blessed are ye, when men shall hate you, and when they shall separate you from their company, and shall reproach you, and cast out your name as evil, for the Son of man's sake.

ROM 13:13 Let us walk honestly, as in the day; not in rioting and drunkenness, not in chambering and wantonness, not in strife and envying. 14 But put ye on the Lord Jesus Christ, and make not provision for the flesh, to fulfil the lusts thereof.

1JO 3:14 We know that we have passed from death unto life, because we love the brethren. He that loveth not his brother abideth in death.

ROM 12:17 Recompense to no man evil for evil. Provide things honest in the sight of all men. 18 If it be possible, as much as lieth in you, live peaceably with all men. 19 Dearly beloved, avenge not yourselves, but rather give place unto wrath: for it is written, Vengeance is mine; I will repay, saith the Lord. 20 Therefore if thine enemy hunger, feed him; if he thirst, give him drink: for in so doing thou shalt heap coals of fire on his head. 21 Be not overcome of evil, but overcome evil with good.

EPH 2:2 Wherein in time past ye walked according to the course of this world, according to the prince of the power of the air, the spirit that now worketh in the children of disobedience: 3 Among whom also we all had our conversation in times past in the lusts of our flesh, fulfilling the desires of the flesh and of the mind; and were by nature the children of wrath, even as others. 4 But God, who is rich in mercy, for his great love wherewith he loved us, 5 Even when we were dead in sins, hath quickened us together with Christ, (by grace ye are saved;) 6 And hath raised us up together, and made us sit together in heavenly places in Christ Jesus: 7 That in the ages to come he might shew the exceeding riches of his grace in his kindness toward us through Christ Jesus.

GAL 5:19 Now the works of the flesh are manifest, which are these; Adultery, fornication, uncleanness, lasciviousness, 20 Idolatry, witchcraft, hatred, variance, emulations, wrath, strife, seditions, heresies, 21 Envyings, murders, drunkenness, revellings, and such like: of the which I tell you before, as I have also told you in time past, that they which do such things shall not inherit the kingdom of God. 22 But the fruit of the Spirit is love, joy, peace, longsuffering, gentleness, goodness, faith, 23 Meekness, temperance: against such there is no law.

EPH 4:26 Be ye angry, and sin not: let not the sun go down upon your wrath: 27 Neither give place to the devil.

Anger, strife, and resentment constrict our thoughts and capture them. We dwell on the person that hurt us and not on God. We wish evil on the person. Our pain or anger pulls our thoughts back to him or her constantly. Our imagination runs to hurtful recompense. We become trapped within our malicious thoughts. It is a trap sprung on us by us and it is difficult to escape.

PSA 94:11 The LORD knoweth the thoughts of man, that they are vanity.

PSA 119:113 I hate vain thoughts: but thy law do I love.

PSA 139:23 Search me, O God, and know my heart: try me, and know my thoughts: 24 And see if there be any wicked way in me, and lead me in the way everlasting. 140:1 Deliver me, O LORD, from the evil man: preserve me from the violent man; 2 Which imagine mischiefs in their heart; continually are they gathered together for war.

JER 6:19 Hear, O earth: behold, I will bring evil upon this people, even the fruit of their thoughts, because they have not hearkened unto my words, nor to my law, but rejected it.

The minimum penalty we can hope for in this state is that our minds will be stripped of God's presence and engorged with resentment and hate. Our beloved will be taken from us by force and replaced with resentment. Our finite minds have only limited capacity and so He will be pushed out when thoughts of anger and resentment become sizable enough the intruders will crowd and push the Lord from our heart. Even if some thought of the Lord remains, the voices of hate and anger are strong and constant enough His sweet voice will not be easily heard.

Our spirit will suffer and starve. Christ is our focus and our bread. He is the food of our soul. It is He who sustains us. Let our minds dwell on the goodness of the Lord. But, be warned, we can be taken by surprise and the enemy can cause wrath and pain at the hands of others. It is not enough to be vigilant. If wounded we must be willing to forgive. Hate, resentment, and anger tie us to the past. God does not live in the past, only in the present.

We know we must forgive and forget, yet, at times it is not so easy. If there are issues to be addressed through counseling, please refer to my previous book, **Christian Counseling: Healing the Tribes of Man.** For now let us examine the spiritual side of forgiveness. It is a matter of trust in God and His plan. In the story of Joseph, son of Jacob, we see a young boy whose brothers were full of envy and hate toward him. The brothers arranged to capture him while he was away from the protection of his father and sell him into slavery. They never heard from him again and assumed he was dead. Joseph was sold as a slave in Egypt where he ended up in the house of the Pharaoh. There he showed his character and intelligence and rose to be Pharaoh's second in command. There came a famine upon the land, which Joseph had foreseen. Joseph had prepared Pharaoh's kingdom for the event. However, his brothers were in their homeland suffering. Not knowing Joseph was alive, they came into Egypt and asked to buy food. They were brought before Joseph.

GEN 45:4 And Joseph said unto his brethren, Come near to me, I pray you. And they came near. And he said, I am Joseph your brother, whom ye sold into Egypt. 5 Now therefore be not grieved, nor angry with yourselves, that ye sold me hither: for God did send me before you to preserve life. 6 For these two years hath the famine been in the land: and yet there are five years, in the which there shall neither be earning nor harvest. 7 And God sent me before you to preserve you a posterity in the earth, and to save your lives by a great deliverance. 8 So now it was not you that sent me hither, but God: and he hath made me a father to Pharaoh, and lord of all his house, and a ruler throughout all the land of Egypt.

102

God will weave His plan and His will into our lives and will bring good out of the evil done to us. This kind of trust is a hard thing. It demands we replace our pain with our trust in Him. He did not say the hurt would stop, but we can be assured the evil and the pain will be used for good. As the steps of a righteous man are ordered by the Lord, so the outcome of evil and pain inflicted on him also is guided by God. Why does God not prevent the fool from hurting the righteous man? Because even the fool has free will to be foolish, else how could they be saved by their faith?

REGRET, GUILT and SHAME

Regret is emotionally looking back over your shoulder. How can you clearly see your destination when you keep your sight behind you?

Regret: mental sorrow or concern for anything, as for past conduct or negligence: remorse: to remember with sorrow: to bewail the loss or want of. Webster's New School and Office Dictionary

Guilt: the state of being liable to a penalty; sin; criminality.   Webster's New School and Office Dictionary

Shame: a painful sensation caused by a sense of guilt, impropriety, or dishonor; cover with disgrace. Webster's New School and Office Dictionary

Unlike guilt, regret may be more focused on what we have not done. The base issue however, may be a lack of belief God is guiding our path. The path we chose may be good and profitable, but the one we did not choose could have been glorious... or deadly. The path we walk may be filled with trials but there is a sense that we are where we need to be. It is impossible to know what decision is best since we can't walk two paths at once. We may be on a path now we do not like, but it has lessons in it no other path would have. Wherever we are, in heaven or in the belly of hell, God is there. He is with us.

Regret comes from not being satisfied with things as they are. Regret is second-guessing yourself or God. Regret comes from an unsettling feeling that we are not where we need to be. It can be tied to guilt very closely if regret is focused on a past sin or wrong done by you. So often we do things and wish we could take them back. Not to have these feelings shows us to be without conscience. To

104

harbor these feelings of the past robs our lives of God's plans now. Regret is wishing things could have been different, ignoring the grace of today.

Even if our ways are difficult today it does not mean God isn't with us. Even if there is failure, it does not mean the Lord does not order, permit, or arrange the lessons learned. He sends us to school as we send our children to schools. Lessons along the way are instructions to the soul. We must trust God is guiding us. Even if we have disobeyed God and taken paths which we were not intended to take, the grace of God will cause the path we are on to converge with the right one somewhere down the road. Things may not be exactly as they would have, had we not diverged, but in God's grace our mission can be fulfilled. Even if we have ultimate faith God will guide our steps, it does not mean we should passively wait for indecision to overtake us and have fate force us onto a path not of our choosing. If we choose not to choose or not to act we are letting the river of life sweep us downstream and wash us up on its shore, as it will. We must have courage, listen to God's voice, or feel His hand guide us then take that course. God does not guide passively. Passivity is guided by fear.

Regret is looking back on those missteps, which can make us miss God-given opportunities in the present. Regret can be avoided by having course, commitment, and trust. It is up to God to make His path known. It is up to us to take it. We make the best choice we can based on seeking God's will. We commit fully to the path. We trust it will lead us to the place God would have us be.

LUK 9:62 And Jesus said unto him, No man, having put his hand to the plough, and looking back, is fit for the kingdom of God.

PSA 37:23 The steps of a good man are ordered by the LORD: and he delighteth in his way. 24 Though he falls, he shall not be utterly cast down: for the LORD upholdeth him with his hand. 25 I have been young, and now am old; yet have I not seen the righteous forsaken, nor his seed begging bread. 26 He is ever merciful, and lendeth; and his seed is blessed.

2SA 23:3 The God of Israel said, the Rock of Israel spake to me, He that ruleth over men must be just, ruling in the fear of God. 4 And he shall be as the light of the morning, when the sun riseth, even a morning without clouds; as the tender grass springing out of the earth by clear shining after rain. 5 Although my house be not so with God; yet he hath made with me an everlasting covenant, ordered in all things, and sure: for this is all my salvation, and all my desire, although he make it not to grow.

Wherever we are, we must keep our vision. To walk a path there must be two things kept in sight at all times; where we are and where we are going. Where we are includes the immediate obstacles, the tangles and briars at our feet, and what it will take to make the next step. Where we are going is our destination. This is the heart of God, His love, His Son, His way.

PRO 29:18 Where there is no vision, the people perish: but he that keepeth the law, happy is he.

No greater restraints exist on our journey to God's heart than those of guilt and shame.

For me, guilt was the great wall, the cement in my shoes, and the handcuffs around my heart. Not just an emotional but also an actual physical ailment keeping me from faith and grace. I simply cannot condense guilt to words. An impossible task. A nearly impossible burden to put down. My guilt was all wrapped up in the fact that my church hurt me very badly as a child and a young person. I may have actually felt more than just anger towards the church. In my mind, I transferred that anger to God. It was the only thing I knew to do at the time, I believe it was the way my subconscious or even my conscious mind tried

106

to protect me from any more pain and disillusionment. So over the years the anger and guilt surrounded me. It became comfortable. If I didn't feel the love of God, I would not feel the hurt and disappointment when God let me down - after all, my church let me down and God was my church. Wasn't He? Joyce Dujardin

At times, guilt and shame can be used as weapons of control by church, family, and others. It is not that we should not feel guilt, but that we should not be controlled or beaten down by it. Guilt heaped on us by others, if accepted, cannot be relieved until the other releases us. This is a fine line since we have the scriptures to guide us and they tell us how to approach others who are in sin. We are not to harp on their sin but to come to them at most three times to turn them away from their sin and back to God. We should be careful not to be enticed by our association into their sin.

If you take a dirty cloth and a clean cloth and rub them together, the clean cloth will always get dirty, but the dirty cloth will never come clean. Be careful with whom you associate. W.R. Lumpkin

Guilt, kept in play, will damage the soul. Guilt is about what you do, but shame is about what you are. Guilt can become shame if the person is not allowed to escape the feeling imposed on him by others. This is because when we have repented, corrected course, and changed our ways but still we have guilt heaped on us, we will eventually assume the error is not in what we did but in who or what we are. When this happens we have crossed the line between guilt and shame. Shame is the most destructive of forces. Our shame caused the death of Christ. It is because of what we are He had to die.

107

PSA 69:6 Let not them that wait on thee, O Lord GOD of hosts, be ashamed for my sake: let not those that seek thee be confounded for my sake, O God of Israel. 7 Because for thy sake I have borne reproach; shame hath covered my face.

PSA 69:19 Thou hast known my reproach, and my shame, and my dishonour: mine adversaries are all before thee. 20 Reproach hath broken my heart; and I am full of heaviness: and I looked for some to take pity, but there was none; and for comforters, but I found none. 21 They gave me also gall for my meat; and in my thirst they gave me vinegar to drink.

I must repeat: **Guilt is about what we do, but shame is about what we are.**

Shame is our condition, but we have no right to put shame on others. Our only right is to know it in ourselves and to understand Christ came that we may be free of shame.

We may be guilty of doing something wrong. This is sin and we are all sinners. We CANNOT bring shame upon another. This would be breaking the only laws Christ commanded us to do; love one another as ourselves. So many of us have been taught we are bad people. This is different from people doing bad things. Indeed, we were bad people before Christ came to free us of ourselves. Our state is still sinful, but no one is more sinful than any other. In this light we shall bring judgment into our lives as we shame another.

MAT 7:1 Judge not, that ye be not judged. 2 For with what judgment ye judge, ye shall be judged: and with what measure ye mete, it shall be measured to you again. 3 And why beholdest thou the mote that is in thy brother's eye, but considerest not the beam that is in thine own eye? 4 Or how wilt thou say to thy brother, Let me pull out the mote out of thine eye; and, behold, a beam is in thine own eye? 5 Thou hypocrite, first cast out the beam out of thine own eye; and then shalt thou see clearly to cast out the mote out of thy brother's eye.

Shame destroys people, for we cannot be free of ourselves. Only Christ can set us free and only He has a right to reveal our shame. We may be guilty of sin but when the sin stops and is confessed the guilt is gone. If there is shame how can we help or correct it? Shame will be forever or until Christ reveals to the shameful ones His love and shows them their own worth in Him. Guilt is about deeds. Shame is about worth. Shame makes us feel unworthy of God's grace to the point we may refuse His salvation. This is why shame is so terrible. The love of Christ overcomes shame by showing us we are capable of being loved by God Himself. That is, if we allow Him into our hearts.

God will deal with any church, minister, counselor, or parent who has used shame to diminish or control a child or member accordingly. If you are controlled by shame you must understand we are all the same sinful creatures and no person is worth more in God's eyes than you are right now. You have complete love and worth in God's eyes, so much so that He would have come and died for you and you alone. If the entire world rejects Him and is damned, He still comes for you.

Christ forgives and forgiveness relieves guilt. Christ transforms us, and this removes shame.

CONDEMNATION, CONVICTION, and JUDGING

One can be convicted without being condemned. Conviction is to be found guilty of a crime or a sin. We are all sinners yet some do not feel convicted. When the Spirit of God reveals to us our shortcomings and our faults we are convicted of them, yet we are not condemned. This is because Christ did not come to condemn us but to save us.

JOH 3:17 For God sent not his Son into the world to condemn the world; but that the world through him might be saved. 18 He that believeth on him is not condemned: but he that believeth not is condemned already, because he hath not believed in the name of the only begotten Son of God. 19 And this is the condemnation, that light is come into the world, and men loved darkness rather than light, because their deeds were evil.

Punishment and darkness is what we will suffer for heaping condemnation on someone else. It is not our place to condemn, only His. Christ is the great judge of all. He will judge and He will convict. If the price of sin has not been paid by believing in Him, then He will condemn. A person's standing with God is not ours to know. We cannot condemn. We cannot convict. We cannot judge the hearts of others.

JOB 21:22 Shall any teach God knowledge? seeing he judgeth those that are high.

JOH 5:22 For the Father judgeth no man, but hath committed all judgment unto the Son:

1CO 4:4 For I know nothing by myself; yet am I not hereby justified: but he that judgeth me is the Lord. 5 Therefore judge nothing before the time, until the Lord come, who both will bring to light the hidden things of darkness, and will make manifest the counsels of the hearts: and then shall every man have praise of God.

110

LUK 23:39 And one of the malefactors which were hanged railed on him, saying, If thou be Christ, save thyself and us. 40 But the other answering rebuked him, saying, Dost not thou fear God, seeing thou art in the same condemnation?

ROM 7:25 I thank God through Jesus Christ our Lord. So then with the mind I myself serve the law of God; but with the flesh the law of sin. 8:1 There is therefore now no condemnation to them which are in Christ Jesus, who walk not after the flesh, but after the Spirit.

JAM 4:11 Speak not evil one of another, brethren. He that speaketh evil of his brother, and judgeth his brother, speaketh evil of the law, and judgeth the law: but if thou judge the law, thou art not a doer of the law, but a judge. 12 There is one lawgiver, who is able to save and to destroy: who art thou that judgest another?

To be convicted of our sins by the Spirit of God is the beginning of grace. It is in this one premier act God draws us to Him. Seeing the truth about ourselves and the need for a redeemer is the first act of freedom. God wishes to forgive us and bring us into a relationship with Him rather than condemn us. Conviction may be painful but it is an act of grace that will save us from condemnation.

JOH 8:3 And the scribes and Pharisees brought unto him a woman taken in adultery; and when they had set her in the midst, 4 They say unto him, Master, this woman was taken in adultery, in the very act. 5 Now Moses in the law commanded us, that such should be stoned: but what sayest thou? 6 this they said, tempting him, that they might have to accuse him. But Jesus stooped down, and with his finger wrote on the ground, as though he heard them not.   7 So when they continued asking him, he lifted up himself, and said unto them, He that is without sin among you, let him first cast a stone at her. 8 And again he stooped down, and wrote on the ground. 9 And they which heard it, being convicted by their own conscience, went out one by one, beginning at the eldest, even unto

111

the last: and Jesus was left alone, and the woman standing in the midst. 10 When Jesus had lifted up himself, and saw none but the woman, he said unto her, Woman, where are those thine accusers? hath no man condemned thee? 11 She said, No man, Lord. And Jesus said unto her, Neither do I condemn thee: go, and sin no more. 12 Then spake Jesus again unto them, saying, I am the light of the world: he that followeth me shall not walk in darkness, but shall have the light of life.

MYSTICISM AND RECIDIVISM

MAT 13:18 Hear ye therefore the parable of the sower. 19 When any one heareth the word of the kingdom, and understandeth it not, then cometh the wicked one, and catcheth away that which was sown in his heart. This is he which received seed by the way side. 20 But he that received the seed into stony places, the same is he that heareth the word, and anon with joy receiveth it;   21 Yet hath he not root in himself, but endureth for a while: for when tribulation or persecution ariseth because of the word, by and by he is offended. 22 He also that received seed among the thorns is he that heareth the word; and the care of this world, and the deceitfulness of riches, choke the word, and he becometh unfruitful. 23 But he that received seed into the good ground is he that heareth the word, and understandeth it; which also beareth fruit, and bringeth forth, some an hundredfold, some sixty, some thirty.

Starting a journey may be easy. Finishing is not. It takes tenacity and a unique stubbornness to complete what is started. The world has tribulations and enticements to sway us from our course. Our roots of desire for God must go deeper than our roots in the world. Although the above passage is usually related to salvation it shows the trials we will go through and has within it a warning. Many fail. Be prepared to endure and push on! Salvation is only the beginning of our journey. Many do not make it to the starting line.

They hear the word and do nothing with it. Then, there are some who receive the word of God and become saved by believing in Jesus Christ. Salvation fully equips us to meet the Lord in heaven, but now, while in this world, we must decide how high up the mountain we wish to climb. Most will start this mystical journey and grow tired of judging themselves. They will fatigue in seeking God. They will become distracted by the world. They will not endure the Dark Night of the Soul. They will hide their emptiness in the pursuits of this world. They will rest at the foot of the mountain. As for me, I wish to

113

climb the mountain and touch the face of God. It is a costly journey. It will cost time, patience, and finally it will demand from us all we are. But, think of what we will have if we can give it all away.

Most who start this journey will repeat the same step over and over. They will begin, weary, fail, wander, come back, and begin again. Caught in the midst between the emptiness they feel and the price they think they must pay to overcome. Like a seven-day fast they abort after the first day, they will walk the same rutted road again and again. This does no good. It gets us no farther than the time before. Let us make a choice before we begin. After the journey is begun it is either mysticism or recidivism.

SALVATION: A STANDING, A STATE OF MIND

The Spirit of God opens our eyes to what we are and who He is. In that instant we are **convicted** in our hearts. We are **guilty** of sins and crimes against God. We **regret** the decisions and choices that lead us to do those things. When we see his righteousness we feel **shame** for being the proud, unrighteous, and sinful creatures we are. He has **judged** us guilty of sin and we stand ready to be **condemned** with no excuse and no justification. Then Jesus comes! "Father God", He says. "I have died for this one and have paid the price for his crime. I have been condemned for him and have suffered death for him that he may live. My blood was spilled that he may be forgiven."

Our acceptance of Christ's death for us **is salvation.** Salvation is attained when we accept Christ's perfect life given in exchange for our imperfect life. We are justified through or because of Him, but we are not exonerated. We are not found innocent. We are found guilty but Jesus Christ has served our sentence. The law no longer has rule over us. The law has been fulfilled because the payment for breaking the law has been upheld and collected. He paid it for me. I am no longer a slave to sin or the law.

From this point on we must live in the present. Those sins of the past are now behind us. They are forgiven. We must only think of them to learn from our mistakes. They should in no way hold us back. We cannot cling to them. It would be like holding on to an anchor. They would drag us down. We cannot hope to carry the guilt and shame. They will impede and exhaust us. Guilt, shame, and regret must all be left at the foot of the cross where Jesus died; the price for our sins was paid. We now stand before God as free persons.

The blood of an innocent man has been given as payment for our crimes against God. His life has paid the price for our sins. The cost of sin is death. Thus He who had no sin was sacrificed to pay the price, for if a sinner died he would only be paying for his own sins. The payment had to be innocent and sinless blood. There is only one man perfect and sinless; Christ Jesus, the Son of God. Now we are cleansed of our sins. Our **standing** is now sinless in the sight of God, yet in this world we are what we were. Not one molecule has changed. Barring a miracle of healing or transfiguration our **state** has not changed; but it will. Now, the Spirit of God has come to indwell us, teach us, lead us, change us. We will never be sinless or perfect, but we can be better instruments of God. Now we can stand before God and commune with Him. Now being made sinless in the sight of God by Christ, who also intervened as mediator and priest on our behalf, we can boldly approach the throne.

HEB 4:14 Seeing then that we have a great high priest, that is passed into the heavens, Jesus the Son of God, let us hold fast our profession. 15 For we have not an high priest which cannot be touched with the feeling of our infirmities; but was in all points tempted like as we are, yet without sin. 16 Let us therefore come boldly unto the throne of grace, that we may obtain mercy, and find grace to help in time of need.

God exists only in the NOW. God is only in the present. We must be here now. This means we can't be held back by regret, guilt, or shame. These things drag our hurting and sorrowful minds back to the past; back to the time and place of the pain and sin. Our minds and hearts must be clear of conviction and condemnation. The clear and clean eternal now is where our God resides. All paths have led us to this one point in time when we can lay all burdens of regret, guilt, and shame aside.

God has brought us here. He set divergent paths on our road of sin and each divergent path has led to Him. When our eyes were opened we cried, "Lord I am guilty and ashamed! What must I do to be saved?" Now our heart yearns to be with the one who loved us enough to save us. Now we seek the beloved! We must not seek Him in the past. We cannot seek Him in the future. We must seek Him in the present by being totally in the present – here – with Him. He is here in the infinite now. We cannot worry about the future. It is a matter of trust. This is not to say we should be lax or dismissive in our work, but we should trust God to make a way for us to make our way. A road will be provided for us to walk.

MAT 6:26 Behold the fowls of the air: for they sow not, neither do they reap, nor gather into barns; yet your heavenly Father feedeth them. Are ye not much better than they?

MAT 6:31 Therefore take no thought, saying, What shall we eat? or, What shall we drink? or, wherewithal shall we be clothed? 32 (For after all these things do the Gentiles seek:) for your heavenly Father knoweth that ye have need of all these things. 33 But seek ye first the kingdom of God, and his righteousness; and all these things shall be added unto you.

LUK 11:13 If ye then, being evil, know how to give good gifts unto your children: how much more shall your heavenly Father give the Holy Spirit to them that ask him?

The past is gone. The future is not yet here. All we have is now. Without looking forward or back, we worship God now. We praise Him for who He is and what is happening now. He is saving us and showering us with His grace, even now. Let us be completely focused on God at this moment, in the ETERNAL NOW.

THE PRESENCE OF GOD

There is the omnipresence of God and the manifest presence of God. Although God is everywhere all the time, we wish His presence manifested in our lives. This can only be done by His permission and through His grace. With eyes opened and heart on fire we understand the sovereignty of God and cry, "GRACE! GRACE! IT IS BY GRACE ALONE!" We were wooed, convicted, and saved from condemnation because He is gracious. He did not have to do it. We did not deserve it, but He did it anyway.

Now what God wants is a relationship with us, as a father would want to love and nurture a child. We know God is everywhere but He only reveals Himself as He wishes. He may manifest through miracles, visions, but through faith He is manifested in our hearts. Visions are splendid, but they pass quickly. Miracles come so seldom. Jesus is in us forever. It is less spectacular than seeing visions. It is not as awe inspiring as a miracle. It is the power of God in salvation and in life changing action. The manifest presence of God is when God reveals Himself to us. We may seek those moments of visions and miracles as if they will give us the faith to believe more deeply, but signs will not change a person. Only God in us will do that. This is the most powerful manifest presence of God.

MAT 12:38 Then certain of the scribes and of the Pharisees answered, saying, Master, we would see a sign from thee. 39 But he answered and said unto them, An evil and adulterous generation seeketh after a sign; and there shall no sign be given to it, but the sign of the prophet Jonas: 40 For as Jonas was three days and three nights in the whale's belly; so shall the Son of man be three days and three nights in the heart of the earth.

MAT 16:1 The Pharisees also with the Sadducees came, and tempting desired him that he would shew them a sign from heaven. 2 He answered and said unto them, When it is evening, ye say, It will be fair weather: for the sky is red.   3 And in the morning, It will be foul weather to day: for the sky is red and lowering. O ye hypocrites, ye can discern the face of the sky; but can ye not discern the signs of the times?

1CO 1:22 For the Jews require a sign, and the Greeks seek after wisdom: 23 But we preach Christ crucified, unto the Jews a stumbling block, and unto the Greeks foolishness; 24 But unto them which are called, both Jews and Greeks, Christ the power of God, and the wisdom of God.

PART FOUR

A PLACE TO PLACE THE MIND

Thoughts, Actions, and Submission

1TI 4:13 Till I come, give attendance to reading, to exhortation, to doctrine. 14 Neglect not the gift that is in thee, which was given thee by prophecy, with the laying on of the hands of the presbytery. 15 Meditate upon these things; give thyself wholly to them; that thy profiting may appear to all.

PSA 63:6 When I remember thee upon my bed, and meditate on thee in the night watches. 7 Because thou hast been my help, therefore in the shadow of thy wings will I rejoice. 8 My soul followeth hard after thee: thy right hand upholdeth me.

PSA 77:12 I will meditate also of all thy work, and talk of thy doings. 13 Thy way, O God, is in the sanctuary: who is so great a God as our God? 14 Thou art the God that doest wonders: thou hast declared thy strength among the people.

At first glance, there is no difference between the meditation techniques of the Zen Buddhist masters and those of the Christian mystics. Both demand the mind be still, quiet, and focused. Both demand we lose ourselves. Both demand patience and dedication. However, there is a great distinction between the two as to where the mind is placed. The teaching of the Eastern mystics directs the student to "go within", "empty themselves", and "center the mind". Concentrate on the center of the body or on the breath. First there is focus on sound or breath, then on the center where the breath arrives, and then even that disappears into nothingness until nothing is left, not even the self; not even nothingness. The students reach inside until in the depth all disappears into all and into nothingness.

For the Christian mystic, enlightenment is not some static state of oneness, as it is to the Eastern mystic. Instead, it is an ongoing and ever-changing, living relationship between God and man. As it is in any healthy relationship we attempt to learn from and take into ourselves the better part from the other. Thus God as both father and beloved leads us, guides us, and teaches us. It is not only the mind, but the heart itself, which is focused on God. We do not seek to disappear but we seek union with Him who is the creator of all, both Him, and us together as lover and beloved. It is a great and total difference between seeking nothingness and seeking God's presence.

It is important to still the mind and stop the chaotic ramblings of thoughts so we may be fully attentive to God. We may find it necessary to implement techniques, which will help us clear and fully focus our minds. This is where the two mystical communities of East and West break. The Christian mystics use the same centering techniques of breath and sound to still and center the mind but the sound is a prayer or word that is meaningful to us in our relationship to God.

After the mind is brought under submission there is a great difference in what happens next. The Eastern mystic focuses the mind inward or more specifically on nothing, while the Christian mystic begins to reach toward the heart of God. There is a blinding yearning to be one with the spirit of God. It is a longing greater than life. Our heart is a room, a temple built for Him. We are waiting for the guest. It is the longing that does the work. We empty out our ideas of God and of ourselves. We want God to be who He is, not what we think He is. We want His fullness, not our limited idea of His fullness. No idea or imaginings can contain even the slightest portion of Him.

We reach for the Spirit without shape or form. We open the gates of our heart wide in anticipation of the arrival of the beloved. We keep the flame of our heart lit and burning, as one would light a candle to bid someone we love to enter. We wait. We wait. We wait and we reach. We reach until we find our limit. We reach until we find our hearts held down and captive under the cloud that separates us from God. It is then we begin to beat against the cloud with all of the ferocity of a lover held inside a room, away from the beloved, against their will. We have reached as high as we can reach. Like a child who holds up his arms for his father, we wait for God to come, reach down, and pick us up. We wait to be gathered into His arms.

Christian Contemplative Prayer is the opening of mind, heart, and soul to God. It is beyond thoughts and words. It is bringing God in us closer than thinking and feeling. The root of all prayer is interior silence. Only mundane and common prayer is of thoughts or feelings expressed in words. Contemplative Prayer is a prayer of silence, an experience of God's presence in us and we in Him. It is experiencing God which transcends the study of Him. Love is an experience.

SON 1:13 A bundle of myrrh is my well-beloved unto me; he shall lie all night betwixt my breasts. 14 My beloved is unto me as a cluster of campfire in the vineyards of Engedi. 15 Behold, thou art fair, my love; behold, thou art fair; thou hast doves' eyes. 16 Behold, thou art fair, my beloved, yea, pleasant: also our bed is green. 17 The beams of our house are cedar, and our rafters of fir. 2:1 I am the rose of Sharon, and the lily of the valleys. 2 As the lily among thorns, so is my love among the daughters. 3 As the apple tree among the trees of the wood, so is my beloved among the sons. I sat down under his shadow with great delight, and his fruit was sweet to my taste. 4 He brought me to the banqueting house, and his banner over me was love. 5 Stay me with flagons, comfort me with apples: for I am sick of love. 6 His left hand is under my head, and his right hand doth embrace me. 7 I charge you, O ye daughters of Jerusalem, by the roes, and by the hinds of the field, that ye stir not up, nor awake my love, till he please. 8 The voice of my beloved! behold, he cometh leaping upon the mountains, skipping upon the hills. 9 My beloved is like a roe or a young hart: behold, he standeth behind our wall, he looketh forth at the windows, shewing himself through the lattice. 10 My beloved spake, and said unto me, Rise up, my love, my fair one, and come away. SON 2:11 For, lo, the winter is past, the rain is over and gone; 12 The flowers appear on the earth; the time of the singing of birds is come, and the voice of the turtle is heard in our land; 13 The fig tree putteth forth her green figs, and the vines with the tender grape give a good smell. Arise, my love, my fair one, and come away. 14 O my dove, that art in the clefts of the rock, in the secret places of the stairs, let me see thy countenance, let me hear thy voice; for sweet is thy voice, and thy countenance is comely.

He is illusive. Our God, our lover, entices us to higher levels as we run after Him, seeking Him. We must keep Him in our hearts day and night. When we sleep He is our breath and the beating of our hearts. When awake we are ever watchful. With every fiber of our being we anticipate our next encounter. We wait and our hearts long for Him. The longing draws us to Him.

SON 3:1 By night on my bed I sought him whom my soul loveth: I sought him, but I found him not. 2 I will rise now, and go about the city in the streets, and in the broad ways I will seek him whom my soul loveth: I sought him, but I found him not. 3 The watchmen that go about the city found me: to whom I said, Saw ye him whom my soul loveth? 4 It was but a little that I passed from them, but I found him whom my soul loveth: I held him, and would not let him go, until I had brought him into my mother's house, and into the chamber of her that conceived me.

We do not turn our minds off, nor do we seek to disappear into nothingness as the Eastern mystics do. We seek Christ, the beloved. We still our hearts and minds to listen for rustle of His footsteps. We sit quietly, yearning for His approach, His breath upon our face, His fragrance as He enters the room, the mist we see covering His presence, the thin blue mist that surrounds Him. Our minds are turned outward to Him. The more quiet our hearts and minds, the sooner we will recognize Him whom we seek.

The pursuit of God will embrace the labor of bringing our total personality into conformity to His. I do not here refer to the act of justification by faith in Christ.

123

I speak of a voluntary exalting of God to His proper station over us and a willing surrender of our whole being to the place of worshipful submission, which the Creator-creature circumstance makes proper... Let no one imagine that he will lose anything of human dignity by this voluntary sell-out of his all to his God. He does not by this degrade himself as a man; rather he finds his right place of high honor as one made in the image of his Creator. His deep disgrace lay in his moral derangement, his unnatural usurpation of the place of God. His honor will be proved by restoring again that stolen throne. In exalting God over all, he finds his own highest honor upheld...We must of necessity be servant to someone, either to God or to sin. The sinner prides himself on his independence, completely overlooking the fact that he is the weak slave of the sins that rule his members. The man who surrenders to Christ exchanges a cruel slave driver for a kind and gentle Master whose yoke is easy and whose burden is light.   A. W. Tozer

TO STILL THE MIND

Let the remembrance of Jesus be present with your every breath. Then indeed you will appreciate the value stillness.   John Climacus

As we begin our time of meditation and prayer we must be careful. We must first still and focus the mind. This first stage, called centering, is somewhat like techniques used in Eastern mysticism. However, objects or words used in our Christian technique should be kept completely Christ centered in their representation. As we sit in meditation and prayer, many times we find our minds in turmoil, with thoughts chasing themselves like a pack of monkeys. We must first have a way of clearing the mind of such thrashing. Before we can pray clearly we must be able to think clearly. Before we can think clearly we must stop the mind from running amok. Even in this preliminary stage of centering it takes about twenty minutes to still the mind.

Excerpts from "Five Types of Thought: By Father Thomas Keating

The most obvious thoughts are superficial ones the imagination grinds out because of its natural propensity for perpetual motion. It is important just to accept them and not pay any undue attention to them.... Sometimes they reach a point where they don't hear it at all...

The second kind of thought occurs when you get interested in something that is happening...This is the kind of thought that calls for some "reaction."... It is important not to be annoyed with yourself if you get involved with these interesting thoughts. Any annoyance that you give in to is another thought, and will take you farther away from the interior silence...

A third kind of thought arises as we sink into deep peace and interior silence. What seem to be brilliant theological insights and marvelous psychological breakthroughs, like tasty bait, are dangled in front of our mind's eye... If you acquiesce to a thought of this nature long enough to fix it in your memory you will be drawn out of the deep, refreshing waters of interior silence.

As you settle into deep peace and freedom from particular thoughts, a desire to reflect on what is happening may arise. You may think, "At last I am getting some place!" or "This feeling is just great... If you let go, you go into deeper interior silence. If you reflect, you come out and have to start over.... As soon as you start to "reflect" on an experience, it is over...The presence of God is like the air we breathe. You can have all you want of it as long as you do not try to take possession of it and hang on to it.

Any form of meditation or prayer that transcends thinking sets off the dynamic of interior purification....one may feel intense anger, sorrow or fear without any relation to the recent past. Once again, the best way to handle them is to return to the sacred word.

Once you grasp the fact that thoughts are not only inevitable, but an integral part of the process of healing and growth initiated by God, you are able to take a positive view of them. Instead of looking at them as painful distractions... Five Types of Thought: By Father Thomas Keating

It is not that we take a "positive approach to the unwanted and noisy thoughts, but we will acquire a passive approach to them. We will learn to dismiss them like twigs on the trail. We will keep walking without as much as noticing them.

126

...the mind should retire into itself, and recall its powers from sensible things, in order to hold pure communion with God, and be clearly illumined by the flashing rays of the Spirit, with no admixture or disturbance of the divine light by anything earthly or clouded, until we come to the source of the effulgence which we enjoy here, and regret and desire are alike stayed, when our mirrors pass away in the light of truth. Gregory of Nazianzus

TO QUIET THE MIND

Before we begin the first steps of meditation we must find a comfortable and undisturbed place. Sit quietly. Close your eyes and relax. Find in your heart a sacred word. In your heart and soul it must have a direct connection with Christ. Let the word be something special to you. Let it be grace, peace, love, hope, charity, or some word that connects you with Christ himself. Or, you may pick out some sacred object such as a cross or painting which you know will draw your heart to Him. Focus your mind and your heart upon this sacred word or object. Do not let it waiver and do not let it go.

It is common that after only a matter of moments your mind will start to wander. You'll find your focus lost, and your mind chasing itself and swirling like a storm. Your thoughts will become scattered and chaotic. Do not fret and do not worry, this is very common. It is the first obstacle to overcome in order to fully pray and meditate upon Him. God waits on the other side of chaos in our minds and hearts. This is the first step in the process of stripping away all of those things that stand in the way between our Lord and ourselves. The mind will protest and complain. It is like a stubborn mule which strains and complains against the bridle. But bridle our minds we must. It will take infinite time and patience simply to learn to quiet and control our minds so that we can pray and meditate wholly on Him.

Why does this little prayer of one syllable pierce the heavens? Surely, because it is offered with a full spirit, in the height and the depth, in the length and the breadth of the spirit of the one who prays. In the height: that is with the full might of the spirit; in the depth: for in this little syllable all the faculties of the spirit are contained; in the length: because if it could always be experienced as it is in that moment, it would cry as it does then; in the breadth: because it desires for all others all that it desires for itself.... St. John of the Cross

128

There are only two things in existence, the creator and created. As our minds become more still and quiet we must continually push out all of the things that try to enter in. We must allow room only for God in our hearts and minds. Whether it is height, depth, blackness, emptiness, or nothingness itself, all things but God must be pushed out of the mind and heart.

These two things that exist -- God and creation are all there is in the universe. Everything that is not God is creation. If we empty our minds and hearts of everything created what is left will be God.

As we focus our minds' eye sharply on the attributes of the ineffable Godhead, we see it as existing beyond everything created. God transcending all intellect, and all beings and is wholly outside any imagined appearance, knowledge and wisdom. "dwelling in light unapproachable."

...it is the easiest exercise of all and most readily accomplished when a soul is helped by grace in this felt desire; otherwise, it would be extraordinarily difficult for you to make this exercise. Do not hang back then, but labour in it until you experience the desire. For when you first begin to undertake it, all that you find is a darkness, a sort of cloud of unknowing; you cannot tell what it is, except that you experience in your will a simple reaching out to God [a naked intent unto God]. This darkness and cloud is always between you and your God, no matter what you do, and it prevents you from seeing him clearly by the light of understanding in your reason, and from experiencing him in sweetness of love in your affection. So set yourself to rest in this darkness as long as you can, always crying out after him whom you love. For if you are to experience him or to see him at all, insofar as it is possible here, it must always be in this cloud and in this darkness. Excerpts from The Cloud of Unknowing (James Walsh trans., New York : Paulist Press, 1981)

129

God is light unapproachable. We cannot gaze on him. We see *"in a glass darkly and know in part" (1 Cor 13:12)*. Deity, God, the Godhead then, is wholly incorporeal, without dimensions or size and not bounded by shape nor perturbed by them.

ROM 8:38 For I am persuaded, that neither death, nor life, nor angels, nor principalities, nor powers, nor things present, nor things to come, 39 Nor height, nor depth, nor any other creature, shall be able to separate us from the love of God, which is in Christ Jesus our Lord.

1 TI 6:16 Who only hath immortality, dwelling in the light which no man can approach unto; whom no man hath seen, nor can see: to whom be honour and power everlasting. Amen.

1 COR 13:12 For now we see through a glass, darkly; but then face to face: now I know in part; but then shall I know even as also I am known.

PHI 3:6 Concerning zeal, persecuting the church; touching the righteousness which is in the law, blameless.7 But what things were gain to me, those I counted loss for Christ. 8 Yea doubtless, and I count all things but loss for the excellence of the knowledge of Christ Jesus my Lord: for whom I have suffered the loss of all things, and do count them but dung, that I may win Christ, 9 And be found in him, not having mine own righteousness, which is of the law, but that which is through the faith of Christ, the righteousness which is of God by faith: 10 That I may know him, and the power of his resurrection, and the fellowship of his sufferings, being made conformable unto his death; 11 If by any means I might attain unto the resurrection of the dead.

Never let the heart cease its cry. Never let it cease its reach for its creator. Day after day this process must be repeated. As we become accustomed to this toil of forgetting all things created, we must continually reach for God with our hearts with every breath we take. Knocking, no, pounding with our heart's cry on the door that stands between God and us. This is called praying without ceasing. Because there is a separation between God and us, it is a great mystery and paradox. Even though He is with us and in us, there stands a veil of "unknowing" whose only key is grace and only door is faith. God himself must lift the veil as He wills.

1TH 5:16 Rejoice evermore. 17 Pray without ceasing. 18 In every thing give thanks: for this is the will of God in Christ Jesus concerning you. 19 Quench not the Spirit. 20 Despise not prophesying. 21 Prove all things; hold fast that which is good. 22 Abstain from all appearance of evil. 23 And the very God of peace sanctify you wholly; and I pray God your whole spirit and soul and body be preserved blameless unto the coming of our Lord Jesus Christ.

In the inner wine cellar I drank of my beloved, and, when I went abroad through all this valley I no longer knew anything, and lost the herd which I was following. St. John of the Cross

Now I occupy my soul and all my energy is in his service. I no longer tend the herd, nor have I any other work now that my every act is love. St. John of the Cross

I want to deliberately and zealously encourage a mighty and ongoing longing for God. The lack of it has brought us to our present low estate. The stiff and wooden quality of our religious lives is a result of our lack of holy desire. Complacency is a deadly foe of all spiritual growth. Acute desire must be present or there will be no manifestation of Christ to His people. He waits to be wanted. Too bad that with many of us He waits so long, so very long, in vain. A.W. Tozer.

131

THE DANGER OF GIFTS

We are told to abandon the exterior world and seek only God, beyond form and imagination. Like brutes, we beat against the wall as if we could make our eyes see or ears hear some eternal image or voice. Longing turns to drive and yearning to impatience as we crash headlong into our limitations. No longer do we truly wait and depend on grace. We lie to ourselves, believing we have some part in this communion apart from our praying and waiting on Him who made us. Even our communion is up to Him.

Yet, our deceitful hearts, eager to be prideful of their accomplishments, will be entrapped along the way by visions and raptures both imagined and real. If imagined, it is our minds refusal to be still and wait upon the Lord. Lying beast that it is, our mind fills in the void we seek with things of its own making. It is our hearts making us believe we have accomplished something special and worthy of pride. If the visions are real in that they do not originate within us, they serve as only signposts on a long journey. By these visions and signs we can be detoured, stopped or even regressed spiritually. Visions and signs are not God. They are only another creation. They are not the creator. The road to the temple is not the temple. The sidewalk to the temple is not the temple. The bell tolling from the temple is not the temple. The stairway is not the temple. The door is not the temple. Do not stop until you reach the temple. Do you seek God? Then dreams and visions are not what you seek. Do not let them distract you from your Lord. If it is the beloved you seek, his voice or fragrance will not do. Only his presence will quench the thirst of the soul.

...They strain themselves, as though they could possibly see inwardly with their bodily eyes and hear inwardly with their ears; and so with all their senses... The result is that the devil has power to fabricate false lights or sounds, sweet smells in their nostrils, wonderful tastes in their mouths and many other strange

ardors and burnings in their bodily breasts or in their entrails... Excerpts from
The Cloud of Unknowing (James Walsh trans., New York : Paulist Press, 1981)

They who are in sins, and worship the creature rather than the Creator, have
their heart in some way ugly and their understanding exceedingly unsightly...
(The Image of God in Man According to Cyril of Alexandria)

...God is in himself so exalted that he is beyond the reach of either knowledge or
desire. Desire extends further than anything that can be grasped by knowledge.
It is wider than the whole of the heavens, than all angels, even though
everything that lives on earth is contained in the spark of a single angel. Desire
is wide, immeasurably so. But nothing that knowledge can grasp or desire can
want, is God. Where knowledge and desire end, there is darkness and there God
shines.   Meister Eckhart

Such a paradox as is presented here could cause one to give up, feeling hopeless and lost. Desire
will drive us to His door, but the door is locked against us. One longs for God and even the longing
can keep us from Him. Desire, in itself is a detriment, driving the mind to buck and run like the mule
it is. At first, we desire the Lord, seeking Him openly, but if our desire could bring Him to us we would
not need grace. There must be nothing of us in this. Our communion with God is in His hands alone.
We can have no control in this union except to present ourselves as a willing sacrifice.

At the point we turn it all over to His divine will, God is there, waiting for us. We realize it all depends
on His grace. It is because of this paradox we have such turmoil and anguish. It is here the soul is
held at a distance from God. The dark night of the soul descends upon us as we work, toil, and suffer
to approach Him. Morning comes only when we give up and place even our approach to Him and
union with Him in His holy hands.

ROM 11:34 For who hath known the mind of the Lord? or who hath been his counsellor? 35 Or who hath first given to him, and it shall be recompensed unto him again? 36 For of him, and through him, and to him, are all things: to whom be glory for ever. Amen. 12:1 I beseech you therefore, brethren, by the mercies of God, that ye present your bodies a living sacrifice, holy, acceptable unto God, which is your reasonable service. 2 And be not conformed to this world: but be ye transformed by the renewing of your mind, that ye may prove what is that good, and acceptable, and perfect, will of God.

PSA 123:1 Unto thee lift I up mine eyes, O thou that dwellest in the heavens. 2 Behold, as the eyes of servants look unto the hand of their masters, and as the eyes of a maiden unto the hand of her mistress; so our eyes wait upon the LORD our God, until that he have mercy upon us.

1 SA 8:17 And I will wait upon the LORD, that hideth his face from the house of Jacob, and I will look for him.

ISA 40:28 Hast thou not known? hast thou not heard, that the everlasting God, the LORD, the Creator of the ends of the earth, fainteth not, neither is weary? there is no searching of his understanding. 29 He giveth power to the faint; and to them that have no might he increaseth strength. 30 Even the youths shall faint and be weary, and the young men shall utterly fall: 31 But they that wait upon the LORD shall renew their strength; they shall mount up with wings as eagles; they shall run, and not be weary; and they shall walk, and not faint.

God is here when we are wholly unaware of it. He is manifest only when and as we are aware of His Presence. On our part there must be surrender to the Spirit of God, for His work it is to show us the Father and the Son. If we co-operate with Him in loving obedience God will manifest Himself to us, and that

manifestation will be the difference between a nominal Christian life and a life radiant with the light of His face.   A. W. Tozer

THE PROBLEM WITH PERSUASION

JOH 6:44 No man can come to me, except the Father which hath sent me draw him: and I will raise him up at the last day. 45 It is written in the prophets, And they shall be all taught of God. Every man therefore that hath heard, and hath learned of the Father, cometh unto me. 46 Not that any man hath seen the Father, save he which is of God, he hath seen the Father. 47 Verily, verily, I say unto you, He that believeth on me hath everlasting life.

It is a business and numbers count. A preacher without notches on his Bible for each soul "he has saved" is no evangelist at all. There is a critical impediment to persuasive preaching. It is indisputably not real.

Through music and rhetoric, emotions are whipped to a boil. The senses are excited. The mind is persuaded. The spirit remains unchanged. Tens of thousands come to the altar every year. They run, crawl, weep, cry, and finally they leave lost. After the emotional release they feel better but soon they fall back into their old ways and are lost for good, having now lost all hope and faith in the promises made by the preacher. Why? Because a man tried to draw them by persuasion while the Spirit of God must draw them by conviction. There is a problem with persuasive preaching. It destroys faith.

It is God who draws us and God who saves us. It is God's hand that leads us home. It is God who meets us and changes us. It is God who heals us. It is God who embraces us in our times of need. It is God who convicts us but does not condemn us. It is God who forgives and cleanses us. It is not a man, a church, or a denomination. It is the Holy Spirit of the Most High God. There is a problem with persuasive preaching. It places the preacher between the sinner and God.

It is our time to be saved only when He opens our eyes to our need of Him. It is only by His grace that we are brought to see our need, our emptiness, our hopeless state. The preacher's words will fade away. The excitement dies down. The music is silent. The preacher has sold us Jesus and persuasion brings buyer's remorse. There is no need of fanfare. Jesus needs only an introducing. His word and His spirit will do the rest. It is not that we should not preach, but we should never manipulate. There is a problem with persuasive preaching. It confuses the preacher's work for God's grace.

This mystical journey is one between man and God. It has nothing to do with anyone else. No preacher can help you, although they may actually hinder you. No church or denomination is your highway or bridge. The timing is the Lord's. The journey is yours. The destination is the heart of God.

PART FIVE

THE DARK NIGHT

In anguish, our soul cries out to God, but He does not answer. In despair we sit alone and empty, in search of Him. We wish to die for Him. We wish to die to self. Our stubborn carnal hearts keep beating. We died because we cannot die. That is to say, we die inside through sin and sorrow because we refuse to die to self. We struggled to lay ourselves down and pick up His Cross, His glory, His life in us. But the old man resists, fighting for each spiritual breath. This "not dying" is agony. We long for Him, waiting for Him with each breath we take, trying to get out of his way. Yet, no matter how we move ourselves we are still in our own way.

The soul cries out but God seems not to hear. Our hearts cry out for the beloved, but He cannot be found. We are poured out like water. Our hearts are like wax melted and running away. We have waited for Him, prayed for Him, meditated on Him, beckoned Him, cried for Him, wept for Him, hurt for Him, and now we are in agony for Him. He is behind the Cloud, we cannot see Him nor can we feel Him. How can one who is everywhere be so far away? But He is. With prayer and desire we beat against the Cloud, the wall that keeps us from God. We cannot get through the wall.

There is no night darker than this. Sorrow is a knife cutting the soul deeper and deeper and so it becomes a bowl, capable of holding more joy when finally there is the joy of His coming. There is no night more sorrowful...but Joy cometh in the morning. We can do nothing but to await the Son. If we endure, this sorrow, this most deep and personal tribulation, will give way to patience and stillness.

LUK 21:19 In your patience possess ye your souls.

Desire will die and obedience will take its place.

138

ROM 6:16 Know ye not, that to whom ye yield yourselves servants to obey, his servants ye are to whom ye obey; whether of sin unto death, or of obedience unto righteousness?

Grace will be shed on us in obedience to God, and our hearts will receive his fullness.

ROM 5:2 By whom also we have access by faith into this grace wherein we stand, and rejoice in hope of the glory of God. 3 And not only so, but we glory in tribulations also: knowing that tribulation worketh patience; 4 And patience, experience; and experience, hope: 5 And hope maketh not ashamed; because the love of God is shed abroad in our hearts by the Holy Ghost which is given unto us. 6 For when we were yet without strength, in due time Christ died for the ungodly. 7 For scarcely for a righteous man will one die: yet peradventure for a good man some would even dare to die. 8 But God commendeth his love toward us, in that, while we were yet sinners, Christ died for us. 9 Much more then, being now justified by his blood, we shall be saved from wrath through Him.

...with no other light or guide than the one that burned in my heart.
The Dark Night by St John of the Cross

Where have you hidden, Beloved, and left me moaning? You fled like the stag after wounding me; I went out calling you but you were gone. Spiritual Canticle by St John of the Cross.

God, who is all perfection, wars against all imperfect habits of the soul, and, purifying the soul with the heat of his flame, he approves its habits from it, and prepares it, so that at last he may enter it and be united with it by his sweet, peaceful, and glorious love, as is the fire when it has entered the wood. St. John of the Cross

What satisfies love best of all is that we be wholly stripped of all repose, whether in strangers, or in friends, or even in love herself. And this is a frightening life love wants, that we must do with the satisfaction of love in order to satisfy love. They who are thus drawn and accepted by love, and fettered by her, are the most indebted to love, and consequently they must continually stand subject to the great power over strong nature, to content her. And that life is miserable beyond all that the human heart can bear. Hadewijch of Antwerp

Our task is to offer ourselves up to God like a clean smooth canvas and not bother ourselves about what the God may choose to paint on it, but, at every moment, feel only for stroke of his brush. It is the same piece of stone. Each blow from the chisel of the sculptor makes it feel -- if it could feel -- as if it were being destroyed. As blow after blow rings down on it, the stone knows nothing about how the sculptor is shaping it. All it's feels is the chisel hacking away at it's, savaging it and mutilating it. Jean Pierre Caussadede

When God is seen in darkness it does not bring a smile to the lips, nor devotion, or ardent love; neither does the body with the soul tremble or move as at other times; the soul sees nothing and everything; the body sleeps and speech is cut off. Angela of Floigno

HEB 11:32 And what shall I more say? for the time would fail me to tell of Gedeon, and of Barak, and of Samson, and of Jephthae; of David also, and Samuel, and of the prophets: 33 Who through faith subdued kingdoms, wrought righteousness, obtained promises, stopped the mouths of lions. 34 Quenched the violence of fire, escaped the edge of the sword, out of weakness were made strong, waxed valiant in fight, turned to flight the armies of the aliens.35 Women received their dead raised

140

to life again: and others were tortured, not accepting deliverance; that they might obtain a better resurrection: 36 And others had trial of cruel mockings and scourgings, yea, moreover of bonds and imprisonment: 37 They were stoned, they were sawn asunder, were tempted, were slain with the sword: they wandered about in sheepskins and goatskins; being destitute, afflicted, tormented; HEB 11:38 (Of whom the world was not worthy:) they wandered in deserts, and in mountains, and in dens and caves of the earth. 39 And these all, having obtained a good report through faith, received not the promise: 40 God having provided some better thing for us, that they without us should not be made perfect. 12:1 Wherefore seeing we also are compassed about with so great a cloud of witnesses, let us lay aside every weight, and the sin which doth so easily beset us, and let us run with patience the race that is set before us, 2 Looking unto Jesus the author and finisher of our faith; who for the joy that was set before Him endured the cross, despising the shame, and is set down at the right hand of the throne of God. 3 For consider him that endured such contradiction of sinners against himself, lest ye be wearied and faint in your minds. 4 Ye have not yet resisted unto blood, striving against sin.

NO PLACE FOR EGO

We are separate and individual creatures, wishing to fit in, wishing to be unique; wishing to be united, wishing to be distinct. We vacillate between the positions, thinking they are opposites. They are not. The wall in our psyche allowing us to distinguish ourselves from others around us is called the ego boundary. Our egos stubbornly refuse to yield, even to God. Pride and self-protection keeps us separate and distinct but we are not complete or whole. The effects of breaching the ego boundary can be seen in those moments of spiritual or sexual bliss. In the union of husband and wife, in those moments of complete tenderness and giving, when distinction between the lover and beloved is lost, and for a space of time it becomes impossible to know where the emotional and physical lines exist between you and the other. There is no fear of losing self but instead a sense of being poured into the other body and soul in a union both separate and together; individual and united, resulting in tears of joy and a river of emotional release as one is being cleansed as if a flood was washing through the soul.

So it is with the union of God and man. When man's ego boundary is finally lowered and man gives himself, even his self-hood, completely up to God. Man and his individuality are not lost but are borne upon the wings of God's love, washing man clean in a river of love. Breaching the ego boundary is a spontaneous act uncontrolled by man. It is made possible by trust and love deep enough to surrender life and self.

BEING BOUND TOGETHER WITH GOD

Bind us together, Lord. Bind us together with cords that can not be broken. From a spiritual song

ROM 8:38 For I am persuaded, that neither death, nor life, nor angels, nor principalities, nor powers, nor things present, nor things to come, 39 Nor height, nor depth, nor any other creature, shall be able to separate us from the love of God, which is in Christ Jesus our Lord.

The eyes of my soul were opened, and I beheld the plenitude of God, wherein I did comprehend the whole world, both here and beyond the sea, and the abyss, and the ocean, and all things. In all these things I beheld naught save the Divine power, in a matter assuredly indescribable; so that through excess of marveling the soul cried with a loud voice, saying, "this whole world is full of God!" .... Angela of Floigno

Yet the creature does not become God, for the union takes place in God through Grace and our homeward turning love: and therefore the creature in its inward contemplation feels the distinction and the otherness between itself in God. John Ruusbroec

Three parts of the Christian life, **Worship, Study, and Prayer (communion)** keep us in touch with God. Three strands making up the cord that ties us to God and keep us reaching upward to Him. They are **Love, Praise, and Gratitude.**

Worship is to seek and know the worth of God. What is He worth? What a strange question, you may say, but the answer underlies our actions. Is He worthy of praise? Is He worthy of our obedience?

143

How about our study, prayers, love, gratitude... Are these areas in balance? One can love someone and not care to be with him. One can commune with someone and not love him. One can be grateful to a stranger. We can praise the actions of someone when we do not know their character. To get to know God we have Worship, Study, and Prayer. To come into His presence we have Love, Praise, and Gratitude. When all three of these attributes are brought to bear in one relationship there is fullness and joy.

Out of the three, gratitude is the most overlooked. In our world we arrogantly presume our looks, intelligence, strength, or cunning are the reasons we have success, house, car, job, health, or position. We are fools. Without thankfulness we come to believe we sustain ourselves by our own hands. What we have and what we believe we deserve takes on larger proportions and greater value than they should. We come to worship the things of this world more than the maker of all things.

ROM 1:21 Because that, when they knew God, they glorified him not as God, neither were thankful; but became vain in their imaginations, and their foolish heart was darkened. 22 Professing themselves to be wise, they became fools, 23 And changed the glory of the uncorruptible God into an image made like to corruptible man, and to birds, and four footed beasts, and creeping things.

For man, from the beginning of his creation, had been entrusted with the reins of his own volitions, with unrestricted movement towards his every desire; for the Deity is free and man had been formed after Him.   (The Image of God in Man According to Cyril of Alexandria)

But, with a heart open and grateful to God we have joy and an enduring relationship.

PSA 100:2 Serve the LORD with gladness: come before his presence with singing. 3 Know ye that the LORD he is God: it is he that hath made us, and not we ourselves; we are his people, and the sheep of his pasture. 4 Enter into his gates with thanksgiving, and into his courts with praise: be thankful unto him, and bless his name. 5 For the LORD is good; his mercy is everlasting; and his truth endureth to all generations. 101:1 I will sing of mercy and judgment: unto thee, O LORD, will I sing.

Out of gratitude and love springs charity. Charity flies forth from a heart filled with thankfulness and gratitude. All things are seen, as they are, a gift from God. We clearly see His love for us. Our hearts are joyous as we share God's gifts to us with others. Charity is the result of gratitude to God and God's love in us toward our fellow man.

COL 3:14 And above all these things put on charity, which is the bond of perfectness. 15 And let the peace of God rule in your hearts, to the which also ye are called in one body; and be ye thankful.

1 COR 13:13 And now abideth faith, hope, charity, these three; but the greatest of these is charity.

What is the secret of finding the treasure? There isn't one. The treasure is everywhere. It is offered to us at every moment and wherever we can find ourselves. (In) All creatures, friends or enemies, for it is ours abundantly, and it courses through every fiber of our body and soul until it reaches the very core of our being. If we open our mouths they will be filled. Jean Pierre Caussadede

Fickle and forgetful is man that he would trip over the truth, or through grace fall headlong into it, and then rush off, forgetting all he had seen, learned, and felt in his deepest part. Not being reminded of the epiphany daily, man creeps into a mode of doubt and counts all of his communion and time with God as the dross of dreams and imaginings. In the dark nights of the soul, it is not knowledge that keeps us alive. It is faith, unshakable and tenacious. Faith trusts God is still there even if He cannot be seen. Faith knows God is there even if He cannot be felt. Faith sees the sun in the midst of night and faith waits for Joy cometh in the morning. Do you have knowledge of this faith? Is your heart fixed on God? Then the bridegroom will come and we will be one, transformed and conformed, we will be one.

PSA 57:7 My heart is fixed, O God, my heart is fixed: I will sing and give praise. 8 Awake up, my glory; awake, psaltery and harp: I myself will awake early. 9 I will praise thee, O Lord, among the people: I will sing unto thee among the nations. 10 For thy mercy is great unto the heavens, and thy truth unto the clouds. 11 Be thou exalted, O God, above the heavens: let thy glory be above all the earth.

But what passes in the union of the Spiritual Marriage is very different. The Lord appears in the centre of the soul, not through an imaginary, but through an intellectual vision ..., just as He appeared to the Apostles, without entering through the door, when He said to them: "Pax vobis" (peace be unto you) the soul, I mean the spirit of this soul, is made one with God, Who, being likewise a Spirit, has been pleased to reveal the love that He has for us by showing to certain persons the extent of that love, so that we may praise His greatness. For He has been pleased to unite Himself with His creature in such a way that they have become like two who cannot be separated from one another: even so He will not separate Himself from her.   Teresa of Avila

... it must not be thought that the faculties and senses and passions are always in this state of peace, though the soul itself is. In the other Mansions *(i.e. those mansions which are exterior to the central one in which the soul now dwells)* there are always times of conflict and trial and weariness, but they are not of such a kind as to rob the soul of its peace and stability -- at least, not as a rule.

146

...for it is difficult to understand how the soul can have trials and afflictions and yet be in peace... Teresa of Avila

... in this temple of God, in this Mansion of His, he and the soul alone have fruition of each other in the deepest silence. There is no reason now for the understanding to stir, or to seek out anything, for the Lord Who created the soul is now pleased to calm it and would have it look, as it were, through a little chink, at what is passing. Now and then it loses sight of it and is unable to see anything; but this is only for a very brief time   Teresa of Avila

And I am quite dazed myself when I observe that, on reaching this state, the soul has no more raptures (accompanied, that is to say, by the suspension of the senses), save very occasionally, and even then it has not the same transports and flights of the spirit. These raptures, too, happen only rarely, and hardly ever in public as they very often did before. Nor have they any connection, as they had before, with great occasions of devotion... Teresa of Avila

It is the nature of the Holy Spirit that I should be consumed in him, dissolved in him, and transformed wholly into love. ... God does not enter those who are freed from all otherness and all createdness: rather he already exits in an essential manner within them... Meister Eckhart

God is always near you and with you; leave Him not alone. ...I continued some years, applying my mind carefully the rest of the day, and even in the midst of my business, *to the presence of God*, whom I considered always *with* me, often *in* me.   Brother Lawrence

... And the latter (union) comes to pass when the two wills -- namely that of the soul and that of God -- are conformed together in one, and there is naught in the one that is repugnant to the other. And thus, when the soul rids itself totally of that which is repugnant to the Divine will and conforms not with it, it is transformed in God through love.   Saint John of the Cross

In thus allowing God to work in it, the soul ... is at once illumined and transformed in God, and God communicates to it His supernatural Being, in such wise that it appears to be God Himself, and has all that God Himself has. And this union comes to pass when God grants the soul this supernatural favour, that all the things of God and the soul are one in participant transformation; and the soul seems to be God rather than a soul, and is indeed God by participation; although it is true that its natural being, though thus transformed, is as distinct from the Being of God as it was before... Saint John of the Cross

JOH 14:18 I will not leave you comfortless: I will come to you. 19 Yet a little while, and the world seeth me no more; but ye see me: because I live, ye shall live also. 20 At that day ye shall know that I am in my Father, and ye in me, and I in you. 21 He that hath my commandments, and keepeth them, he it is that loveth me: and he that loveth me shall be loved of my Father, and I will love him, and will manifest myself to him.

JOH 15:4 Abide in me, and I in you. As the branch cannot bear fruit of itself, except it abide in the vine; no more can ye, except ye abide in me. 5 I am the vine, ye are the branches: He that abideth in me, and I in him, the same bringeth forth much fruit: for without me ye can do nothing.

To abide in the one we love, what bliss this is. In the sense of husband and wife and as lover and beloved, to be in the presence of the one whom your soul loves heals and extends the soul. It fills and fulfills the soul and by this there is no more need for expressions of ecstasy because ecstasy is here. Expressions of ecstasy come as we are reaching for or entering it. When there, we become quiet and peaceful, wanting nothing more than to remain. To stay, to look upon the face of the beloved, to remain in the embrace, being bound together with God brings peace passing all understanding.

IN THIS LIFE

From a young age I thought the contemplative life would best suit those like me, but there was nowhere to go. Protestants do not have a place set aside for the contemplative. They are expected to find a way to live in the "real world". The church never addresses this path nor teaches us how to live it out in the harried world of today. Possibly they do not know. Certain lay groups have come into existence to fill the void left by the church itself. Groups like the Upper Room, the Emmaus Walk, and other Christian ministries and retreats give us insight into other ways of worship. They awaken a deeper desire for God, but they are a temporary change of venue. Most retreats last less than a week.

All of these give us insight into the heart of God. However, they cannot teach us to live toward this end since there is not time to establish a discipline or pattern for life in only a few days. They seek only to spark a hunger. To reach toward the heart of God one must first realize the intense emptiness within, even in the midst of this land of plenty. One must attempt to plumb the depths of their own heart and find it selfish, unworthy, and vile, even as others may admire or praise you. Lastly, vision of the true worth and presence of God must be sought. He should be sought without wavier but as humans we cannot be stable, steadfast, or pure. We must rely on His grace to draw us to Him.

The contemplative life in a modern world is one of walking introspection and self-observation. As we come to understand how truly sinful we are, we also come to understand the vastness of His grace and gift to us. As we watch our thoughts and actions closely and ask why we act and think as we do we will see all we are grows from a root of selfishness and pride.

What possible good could we do for God? None. He loves us in spite of what we are. This is grace.

The contemplative life in this rushed and demanding world is one of continual prayer and upward reaching to God. Beyond the basic doctrine discussed in this little work, and beyond the thoughts and understanding of man waits the embrace of God. Do not let your mind become muddled or confused in meaningless doctrine or debate. Do you know Jesus is the Son of God? Do you know He was born of a virgin, sinless, lived, and died for the sins of the world, including yours? Do you know you are forgiven through your faith in Christ? This begins our relationship with God. Now it is up to us to love Him and pursue Him as the beloved of our heart. It cannot be any more complicated than this. Even a child should be able to understand the Gospel, the good news. Jesus commanded us to permit the little children to come to him. Then He commanded us to have the heart of a child; simple, direct, open, and loving. He told us to simply have faith in Him.

There is wisdom in not relying on our own knowledge and abilities. There is wisdom in insecurity. We cannot assume we understand the heart and mind of God. We must continue to seek Him and seek His wisdom for us.

PRO 3:5 Trust in the LORD with all thine heart; and lean not unto thine own understanding. 6 In all thy ways acknowledge him, and he shall direct thy paths. 7 Be not wise in thine own eyes: fear the LORD, and depart from evil.

There are none more dangerous than people or denominations who believe they have the entire truth. There are none so proud and in error as those who believe they have the only way. If a church believes they are "The Way" they have supplanted even Christ.

JOH 14:6 Jesus saith unto him, I am the way, the truth, and the life: no man cometh unto the father, but by me. 7 If ye had known me, ye should have known my Father also: and from henceforth ye know him, and have seen him.

The contemplative man seeks God and not some "way". He seeks to know and love God more each day. It is not about some formula of baptism, names, titles, or membership. It is about seeking the face of God.

This contemplative life demands patience. We rely on the grace of God. Although we continually knock on the door of heaven with the urgings of our heart toward Him, it is up to God to open the door. We never know when we will knock and grace will open the door. We never know what God has in store for us when grace opens the door. It could be a calming breeze to our soul, a vision of hell, or God's overwhelming presence. To exemplify this I will tell you about a personal event.

Visions may be an expression of what the spirit can communicate in no other way. Certainly, there would be no need for visions and dreams if we were fully aware of those things of God. If we were fully His or could see Him or hear Him we would know those things which visions reveal to our dull hearts and minds. Visions are gifts for those who could not see any other way.

I once saw a vision, vivid as day. Walking in the woods, praying, and in spiritual pain, I came into a clearing. I looked up to see a wall of transparent blocks twelve feet high and twenty feel long. Through the wall I saw a mob of creatures, terrible and fierce, coming at me to destroy me. They looked to be an army of demons. Above the wall hovered an angel with a large pitcher in his hand. He began to pour a deep red liquid into the wall, filling it up as if it were hollow. The demons crashed into the wall, bouncing off, wincing in pain, unable to penetrate the wall, hitting it again and again to no avail. I looked at the angel, frightened and astonished. "The Blood of Christ is protecting you." He said. I knew what I was seeing was taking place in my life on a spiritual level I could not see. The burden of worry I had been carrying lifted from me and I fell to my knees and sobbed.

Wounded by love and stunned by grace, I was transfixed and unmoving, feeling the arms of God around my soul, I wanted nothing more than to stay.

We never know when we will be surprised by grace. Even if it never happens He is still God. We may never hear His voice or sense His presence, but He is still God. To know this is to live in Him. To recognize it is to have the manifest presence of God in our life.

In this life where we seek the love of God, we may meet Him along the way from time to time. When man meets God he is changed forever, but even if he does not meet God in a manifest way, man is still changed because God is slowly working in a personal way within our hearts right now. To be completely aware of His presence in our life will have the same effect as any manifestation because at that moment of realization He is manifest to you. The realization of God is the manifestation of God. Although it may not be in pillars of smoke and fire, we see Him in our lives, in our hearts, and in our world. Our souls exclaim:

PSA 8:1 O LORD, our Lord, how excellent is thy name in all the earth! ...

This is not to be found in the "religious" life. Liturgy, ceremony, repetition, prayers, yantra, mantra, movement, nor deprivation will bring us one step closer to Him. He is found in the searching. He is found in the desire to know Him. He is found in the depth of our love of Him.

(Those who would be partakers of eternal life) must further possess a vigilant and wakeful mind, distinguished by the knowledge of the truth, and richly endowed with the radiance of the vision of God; so as for them, rejoicing therein, to say *Thou, O Lord, will light my lamp: Thou, my God, wilt lighten my darkness* . Cyril of Alexandria

... It is our duty, therefore, to draw near to the true light, even Christ, praising Him in psalms and saying, *Lighten mine eye, that I sleep not for death*... Let,

153

therefore, our loins be girt, and our lamps burning, according to what has been spoken unto us.   Cyril of Alexandria

(The Son) Himself shed the divine and spiritual light on those whose heart was darkened; for which reason He said, *I am come a light into this world*). Cyril of Alexandria

Oh, union of unity, demanded of God by Jesus Christ for men and merited by him! How strong is this in a soul that is become lost in its God! After the consummation of this divine unity, the soul remains hid with Christ in God. This happy loss is not like those transient ones which ecstacy operates, which are rather an absorption than union because the soul afterwards finds itself again with all its own dispositions. Here she feels that prayer fulfilled -- John 17:21: "That they all may be one as thou Father art in me, and I in thee; that they also may be one in us." Jeanne-Marie Bouvier de la Motte-Guyon

PSA 8:1...who hast set thy glory above the heavens.

PSA 18:46 The LORD liveth; and blessed be my rock; and let the God of my salvation be exalted.

PSA 34:3 O magnify the LORD with me, and let us exalt his name together.

PSA 34:8 O taste and see that the LORD is good: blessed is the man that trusteth in him.

PSA 40:1 I waited patiently for the LORD; and he inclined unto me, and heard my cry. 2 He brought me up also out of an horrible pit, out of the miry clay, and

set my feet upon a rock, and established my goings. 3 And he hath put a new song in my mouth, even praise unto our God: many shall see it, and fear, and shall trust in the LORD.

ISA 40:31 But they that wait upon the LORD shall renew their strength; they shall mount up with wings as eagles; they shall run, and not be weary; and they shall walk, and not faint. 41:1 Keep silence before me, O islands; and let the people renew their strength:

Is this not the mystical life? Is this not the life we seek?

THE CONCLUSION

ECC 12:10 The preacher sought to find out acceptable words: and that which was written was upright, even words of truth. 11 The words of the wise are as goads, and as nails fastened by the masters of assemblies, which are given from one shepherd. 12 And further, by these, my son, be admonished: of making many books there is no end; and much study is a weariness of the flesh. 13 Let us hear the conclusion of the whole matter: Fear God, and keep his commandments: for this is the whole duty of man. 14 For God shall bring every work into judgment, with every secret thing, whether it be good, or whether it be evil.

As I struggled to find a place to end this work it became obvious there was no ending. We may plumb the depths of the ocean, because they are deep but finite. We may look out to the stars -the distance is vast but can be measured. How then can we presume to define an ending for that one thing which we know to be infinite, immeasurable, and everlasting? What can be said except the journey is for a lifetime and forever beyond. Let us hear a conclusion. There is none but to Love God, Love others, do His will, seek after Him with all of your heart, and all will be good with your soul.

BIBLIOGRAPHY

The Bible. King James Version, unless otherwise noted.

Burghardt, Walter J., S.J. The Image of God in Man according to Cyril of Alexandria. Washington: Catholic University of America Press, 1957.

Cyril of Alexandria. Commentary on the Gospel of St. Luke. Trans. Robert Payne Smith. United States: Studion Publishers, 1983.

Cyril of Alexandria. Cyril of Alexandria: Select Letters. Trans. Lionel R. Wickham. Oxford: Oxford University Press, 1983.

Cyril of Alexandria. On the Unity of Christ. Trans. John Anthony McGuckin. Crestwood, NY: St. Vladimir's Seminary Press, 1995.

The sayings of the Desert Fathers : the alphabetical collection. Trans. Benedicta Ward, SLG. Kalamazoo, Michigan: Cistercian Publications Inc., 1984, 1975.

Gregory of Nazianzus. Orations. Trans. under the editorial supervision of Philip Schaff and Henry Wace.

International Consultation on English Texts (ICET) and the English Language Liturgical Consultation (ELLC)

John Climacus. The Ladder of Divine Ascent. Trans. Colm Luibheid and Norman Russell. Mahwah, New Jersey: Paulist Press, 1982.

The Lenten Triodion, liturgical prayers recited by the Eastern Orthodox Church during the season of Lent. The nten Triodion. Trans. The Community of the Holy Myrrbearers. The Lenten Triodion. Trans. Mother Mary and Archimandrite Kallistos Ware. London: Faber and Faber, 1977.

St. Nikodimos of the Holy Mountain and St. Makarios of Corinth. The Philokalia, The Complete Text. Trans. G.E.H. Palmer; Philip Sherrard; and Kallistos Ware. London: Faber and Faber Limited, (Vol. 1) 1979, (Vol. 2) 1981

Symeon the New Theologian. Symeon the New Theologian: The Discourses. Trans. C.J. de Catanzaro. Ramsey, N.J.: Paulist Press, 1980. Symeon the New Theologian. On the Mystical Life: The Ethical Discourses. Trans. Alexander Golitzin. Crestwood, NY: St. Vladimir's Seminary Press, 1996.

Angela of Foligno. Angela of Foligno: Complete Works. Mahwah, New Jersey: Paulist Press, 1993.

Anonymous. The Cloud of Unknowing and Other Works. Trans. Clifton Wolters. New York: Penguin Books USA, Inc., 1961, 1978.

Catherine of Siena. Catherine of Siena: The Dialogue.Trans. Suzanne Noffke, O.P. Mahwah, New Jersey: Paulist Press, 1980.

St. John of the Cross, a Spanish Mystic, who lived from 1542 to 1591. John of the Cross. Ascent of Mount Carmel. Trans. E. Allison Peers.

Julian of Norwich, an English mystic who lived from 1342 to 1413. Julian of Norwich. Revelations of Divine Love. Ed. Grace Warrack

Brother Lawrence of the Resurrection. The Practice of the Presence of God. Mount Vernon, NY: Peter Pauper Press, Inc., 1963.

Bonaventure by Ewert Cousins Mahwah, New Jersey: Paulist Press, 1978

Thomas Merton. Thoughts in solitude. Boston: Shambhala Publications, Inc., 1956, 1958.

Nicholas of Cusa. Nicholas of Cusa: Selected Spiritual Writings. Trans. Hugh Lawrence Bond. Mahwah, New Jersey: Paulist Press, 1997.

Teresa of Avila. Interior Castle. Trans. E. Allison Peers. New York: Bantam Doubleday Dell Publishing Group, Inc., 1990.

Teachings of the Christian Mystics by Andrew Harvey; Shambala Boston and London

Thomas à Kempis. The Imitation of Christ. Trans. Richard Whitford, moderenized by Harold C. Gardiner. New York: Doubleday, 1955.

Jacob Boehme. The Supersensual Life. Trans. William Law.

A. W. Tozer. The Pursuit of God. Wheaton, Ill.: Tyndale House, 1982.

Meister Eckhart. Meister Eckhart: Selected Writings. Trans. Oliver Davies. New York: Penguin Books USA, Inc., 1994.

Jeanne-Marie Bouvier de la Motte-Guyon. Autobiography of Madame Guyon.

Marguerite Porete. Marguerite Porete: The Mirror of Simple Souls. Trans. Ellen L. Babinsky. Mahwah, New Jersey: Paulist Press, 1993.

Mysticism in World Religions   by Deb Platt

Wikipedia, the free encyclopedia.

W.R. Lumpkin A Southern Baptist pastor of more than 25 years.

Look for other fine books by Joseph Lumpkin.

The Lost Book Of Enoch: A Comprehensive Transliteration
By Joseph Lumpkin
ISBN: 0974633666

The Gospel of Thomas: A Contemporary Translation
By Joseph Lumpkin
ISBN: 0976823349

Christian Counseling: Healing the Tribes of Man
By Joseph Lumpkin
ISBN: 1933589970

The Tao Te Ching: A Contemporary Translation
By Joseph Lumpkin
ISBN: 0976823314

The Book of Jubilees; The Little Genesis, The Apocalypse of Moses
By Joseph Lumpkin
ISBN 1933580097